I0552225

ISBN-978-1-940087-67-2

21 Crows Dusk to Dawn Publishing, 21 Crows, LLC

Always follow the rules/regulations in the areas you explore. Do not trespass. Do not enter areas after dark if it is not allowed—most parks are open dawn to dusk, but check times before entering. The information in this book like addresses are given to show where the story is located. Please check property ownership before visiting.

Table of Contents

Southeast

Hocking State Forest Balanced Rock Trails   8
Devil's Tea Table

Old Man's Cave Hocking Hills State Park   10
The Baying Hound of Old Man's Cave

Ash Cave   14
Vanishing Hiker of Ash Cave

Cedar Falls   18
The Road to Hell

Moonville Tunnel   20
The Darker Side of Moonville

Moonville Tunnel   22
Rabbit. Rabbit.

King Hollow/Mineral Tunnel   24
The Eight Foot Ghost of King Hollow Tunnel

West State Street Cemetery   29
Weeping Angel

Athens Lunatic Asylum Cemetery Trail   31
The Old Asylum Ghosts

Lake Hope State Park   38
Night Watchman

Airplane Hollow   40
The Legend of Airplane Hollow: IT Calls Things In

Richland Furnace   44
Ghosts in the Old Richland Furnace Ghost Town

Union Cemetery   46
Elizabeth's Grave

Dillon Falls   49
Ghost of the Old Quaker Burial Ground

Table of Contents

Southwest

John Rankin House 53
Ghostly Steps toward Freedom

Cincinnati Music Hall 55
The Dead Don't Rest

Five Rivers Metroparks Island Metropark 57
The Ghost of Bessie Little Bridge

Alexandria Point 61
White Lady Point

Richardson Forest Preserve 63
Lick Road—The Legend of Amy

Darby-Lee Historic Cemetery 64
The Legend of the Fiddler Green

Halfway Between Plainville and Red Bank 66
The Ghost of Newell's Hollow

Château Laroche The Loveland Castle Museum 68
Loveland Castle

Old Lafferty Road and Chicken Hollow Road 71
Calico Lady of Chicken Hollow

Dead Mans Hollow 75
Dead Mans Hollow

Hills and Dales Metropark 78
Frankenstein's Castle

An Old Woods in Denver 80
The Ella Light

Bridge Over Ohio Brush Creek 82
The Strange Demise of Julia Eichel

Great Miami River Recreational Trail 84
Ghost Among the Corpses

Ghost Hollow 86
A Place Called Ghost Hollow

Table of Contents

Mid-Ohio

Little Pennsylvania Cemetery   89
About Wooly Booger Cemetery (or whatever it is
called)

Otterbein United Methodist Church Cemetery   91
Bloody Horseshoe Grave

Stages Pond State Nature Preserve   95
Dead Mules Rising

Still-house Hollow   97
A Place Called Still-house Hollow

Muddy Prairie Run   100
Ghostly Old Man on a Mule with a Keg of Rum

Old Logan Road SE   102
Dead Peddler of Sugar Grove

Allen's Knob   104
Allen's Knob Lone Grave

Schiller Park German Village   107
Headless Man of Schiller Park

Table of Contents
Northeast

Erie Street Cemetery 110
Joc-O-Sot

Cuyahoga County Jackass Hill 111
Cleveland's Mad Butcher

Ohio State Reformatory 113
Prison of the Dead

Lyons Falls Mohican State Park 115
The Legend of Lyons Falls

Elliot Family Farmstead & Cemetery -West Branch 117
State Park
Witch's Grave

Beaver Creek State Park Jake's Lock 120
Jake's Lock: Dead Night Watchman

Beaver Creek State Park Gretchen's Lock 121
Gretchen's Lock

Beaver Creek State Park Hambleton's Mill 123
The Ghost of Esther Hale

Blue Bridge 125
The Grim Apparition at Blue Bridge of Samuel
Seymour

Salem Reformed Cemetery 127
Angel of Death

Ruins of Swift Mansion - Light and Hope 129
Orphanage
Gore Orphanage

Louiza Catherine Fox Murder Site 131
IT Came

Coshocton Along the Panhandle 135
The Old Oak Tree

Bridge over Sugar Creek 137
The Sack Did Rise As Did the Ghost

Table of Contents

Northwest

Put-In-Bay 140
The Gray Ghost

Fallen Timbers Battlefield 141
Ghosts of Fallen Timbers Battlefield

Buckland Lock 143
Bill Bellington Won't Leave Buckland's Lock

Lock 14 Miami & Erie Canal 145
Bloody Bridge

Dr. Martin Luther King Jr. Bridge The Old Cherry 148
Street Bridge
Plodding Ghost of Dr. Martin Luther King Jr. Bridge

Goll Woods State Nature Preserve 149
The Feu Follet of Goll Woods

Goll Woods State Nature Preserve & Cemetery 151
Shhh! Don't Awaken Marieanne

Bridge over Muddy Creek 152
Elmore Rider

Republic Train Tracks 154
The Warning Light

Harrod Cemetery and Highway 56 156
Hatchet Man

For Those Who Like to Seek Out Ghosts

Energy and Seeking Out Ghostly Activity 159

It is All About the Respect and Research 160

Simple Tools to Seek Out Ghosts 161

Things That Go Bump in the Night 167

Citations

Southeast Ohio

> ## *Hocking State Forest*
> ## *Balanced Rock Trails*
> *Rock Climbing/Rappelling Lot*
> *24798 Big Pine Road*
> *Logan, Ohio 43138*
> *Parking: 39.458883, -82.558475*
> *Cross Big Pine Road and then the small bridge. After crossing the bridge, take the trail to the left, following blue Buckeye Trail blazes. Rock will be about 0.6 miles & across from wooden horse tie posts.*

Devil's Tea Table

Devil's Tea Table.

Not far from Old Man's Cave and Conkle's Hollow, there is a trail leading deep into the forest. If you turn right, you will find yourself at one of Ohio's tallest waterfalls, Big Springs. If you turn left, you may wish you had not because there is a huge rock formation among the cliffs not far along the path called a Devil's Tea Table. Now, scientifically speaking, the stone is caused by the area's sandstone, a loose conglomerate (mixture) of layered hard and soft materials.

The rock balanced on top is a harder seam of sandstone than the base. The base or pillar holding it is a looser conglomerate easily eroded by water, creating the illusion of a balanced stone on top. But as far as folklore, settlers of old passed along that on full moon nights, the devil danced upon these stones. If you made eye contact, he could steal your soul!

Old Man's Cave
Hocking Hills State Park
OH-664
Logan, Ohio 43138
39.438049, -82.537987

The Baying Hound of Old Man's Cave

Old Man's Cave in earlier times.

The little town of Cedar Grove, once a farming community between Logan and South Bloomingville, is settled near a sandstone gorge with a meandering stream called Cedar Creek running beneath high cliffs. For over 150 years, locals have complained of a ghost wandering through the valley below. It is bothersome, in the least, as it is a baying hound and sometimes is accompanied by its owner.

It was seen and heard by many, but the most famous sighting was one of its first when two little fellows in the mid-1800s came upon a large recess cave in their explorations one warm afternoon and decided to light a small campfire, maybe just because they could as neither of their parents were around.

It might have been the scent of burning wood that awakened the ghost, or it could have been the rowdiness of the two little boys playing within. Whatever it was, we don't know and probably never will, but as the boys sat around their fire, a ghostly apparition appeared and walked right past them. It was an aged man with a long, gray beard, old-fashioned leather clothing, and moccasins. He carried an antique rifle over his shoulder, and a tall, white hound dog walked by his side. The old man stopped just steps away from the slack-mouthed, shocked boys and disappeared into the cave's sandy bottom. The boys immediately sought help from their elders, who dug up the cave floor only to find two sets of bones—a man and a dog, an old flintlock rifle with the date of 1702 etched into the wood, and some cooking pots. There was also a scratching in the stone that stated the man's name as Retzler, his dog as Harper, and the date of their death as 1777.

For quite some time, many travelers would visit to see the bones inside the cave they dubbed Dead Man's Cave or Old Man's Cave. They would stare down at them and wonder who the man and dog had once been. Whenever a baying hound was heard after that, those in the town above knew they had unsettled the ghosts. They got together and decided to let them rest. After a while, the bones disappeared, and few knew that the townspeople had secretly buried the remains of the old man and his dog to settle the ghosts' unrest. The curious stopped coming, and the story faded away. Yet, the baying of the hound continued.

In the fall of one year, a park ranger at Hocking Hills State Park set out to track down a dog barking in the gorge, believing that poachers were down in the woods below the place called Old Man's Cave. He snatched up his flashlight and worked his way down the rugged trail and deep into the bowels of the gorge, pursuing the hound's crying howl.

However, even as he got closer to the baying and it surrounded him as if twenty dogs were around, he saw nothing in the beam of his flashlight. It circled, and it backed off; it came at him and then faded away. Then suddenly, a certain calm came over the valley. The baying hound had vanished.

Old Man's Cave today—

Many have heard the baying of a phantom dog in the gorge and cave area called Old Man's Cave. In the autumn ten years past and on a park-sanctioned ghost hunt at dusk near Rose Lake, a beautiful fishing area below the campground, I was setting up equipment for about 50 visitors on the dam. Suddenly, below us, near the spillway, came an explosion of barks and howls that broke the quiet air, but no dogs emerged from the woodland. Then they faded away as if the ghostly hound had fled into the forest below, disappearing. Some in the ghost hunting group that night had been skeptics, but became unwavering believers after that. I knew all along that the ghost was there as its presence has long been explained like this—

Before the settling of the town above the dam at Rose Lake, seasonal trappers visited along Cedar Creek, making temporary homes of wood or using the cliff caves as shelters. Each year, they would return to the areas to hunt, fish, and trade stories with each other from the past year.

However, one winter, upon returning, trappers noticed that one among them named Retzler, who made his home in a cave outcropping along with his dog Harper had not been seen for quite some time. The usually heavily traveled path to his lodgings was overgrown, and there was no sign of his faithful hound, who bayed whenever someone neared the camp.

After taking the footpath that led to the cave, they lifted the flap of his leather-hide tent and peered inside. Before them lay the dead trapper along with his old hound dog dead by his side. They carefully lifted the limp bodies of the man and dog and placed them in a shallow hole they had dug in the back of the cave and covered them with sand. And the rest is all history—well, except for the part of the ghosts because they are still around!

The area of Rose Lake where howls have also been heard.

Ash Cave
Hocking Hills State Park
27292 OH-56
South Bloomingville, Ohio 43152
39.395993, -82.545927

Vanishing Hiker of Ash Cave

Ash Cave, named for the large amount of ashes early settlers found piled high on the sand floor of the recess cave and considered to be the remnants of ancient campfires.

Early one spring, Pat Quackenbush, park naturalist, led hikers on a special night tour. It was a short hike along a concrete walkway a half-mile to one particularly large recess in the sandstone called Ash Cave, where a waterfall cascades down a cliff.

It was a small group of twelve people, and this night as they walked, he would pause beneath the hemlocks and cliffs and face the group, pointing out unique features along the route. Each time they stopped, he would make a quick headcount silently to himself to make sure everyone kept up with him. He did not want anyone lost in the dark! "—*ten, eleven, twelve*—" Once Pat could see he had accounted for everyone, he called attention to a deer almost hidden and grazing in the grass. He then piped up with a barred owl's call that, almost immediately, was returned with a couple of hoots from deep in the forest.

He always paused before each stop; there were usually one or two stragglers in the line who would get caught up in the charm of the fairyland-like trail. "—*ten, eleven,*" he counted in his head. "*Yep—twelve. All there.*" And, if needed, Pat would patiently wait for a minute or two, so anyone left behind could catch up before he doled out another trinket or two about the unique area around them.

I used to volunteer at the park, taking the rear of hiking groups to ensure everyone kept up. One time, an old friend showed up and hiked along with me. We were whisper-chatting at the little cave just before the larger Ash Cave while the naturalist noted something about bats there to the crowd. We heard a loud "Shhh!" behind us. There was nobody there. We were shushed by a ghost!

About a quarter of the way, he realized that one dawdler had seemed to creep from the shadows right before he started his spiel. "*—ten, eleven, twelve—and,*" he counted. "*Hmmm, thirteen?*" At first, Pat thought perhaps he had counted the number of people wrong when they met. Maybe this extra hiker had been enjoying the walk alone under the huge hemlocks and wanted some time away from the rest of the group. It was not as troubling that there was one *more* person added to the group than there was one *less*. So instead of waiting and making a recount, the naturalist decided to continue, knowing the straggler would eventually catch up with the group.

Pat along the trail with a group near the spot that a peculiar hiker has been known to join the group.

He was about halfway to the cave when he stopped long enough to talk about an ancient beech tree near the trail. The group had made a half-circle around him, and while they did, he made a great effort to count everyone quickly. "*—ten, eleven, twelve——*" He glanced up and noticed the straggler was only about five feet from the hikers. "*Thirteen!*" He had counted correctly!

But number thirteen was not like the rest. He noted she was wearing old-fashioned clothing—a feed sack dress commonly worn by the thrifty women in the 19th-century depression era who used flour and feed sacks to make their clothing. The mysterious guest was so out-of-place with the group, he was thrown off-guard and simply brought it to everyone's attention. "I turned my attention behind the group," Pat said, "and proceeded to ask if they could see the woman who was standing there and had been following us. I watched them reluctantly turn, and there were more than a few gasps. I wasn't alone. Everyone on that hike saw her." Then she took two steps and disappeared into the woods.

There is quite a lot of speculation of the identity of the ghostly lady at Ash Cave. Some believe it is a woman who lived in a house across the road who visited the cave often and now returns in ghostly form to walk the area she loved. But no one knows who it is for sure. The cave's shelter has been used by traveling Native Peoples, early settlers as a home, and local preachers once held camp meetings at the cave, as above. The cave provided great acoustics, especially from one large stone where preachers stood which was dubbed Pulpit Rock.

Cedar Falls
Hocking Hills State Park
21724 Ohio 374 Scenic
Logan, Ohio 43138
39.418265, -82.526295

The Road to Hell 1782

Cedar Falls—Where screams are heard—

Those hiking in the Hocking Hills may come upon some spirits. Of course, Old Man Retzler and his baying hound are known to show up at Old Man's Cave, and the Pale Lady follows hikers at Ash Cave. But between the two areas, the trail will lead along Queer Creek and to Cedar Falls, where ghosts are said to tarry. Their peculiar screams are explained as this: In the early 1800s, a mill powered by the waters of Queer Creek sat on the rim of Cedar Falls. Nearby was a massive beech tree with words engraved in its ancient trunk, "This is the road to hell, 1782."

The tree was along a dark, tree-covered pathway that worked its way deep into the gorge. It was often used by Shawnee traveling to Chillicothe when tempers were high between settlers and Shawnee. It was speculated often by those visiting the mill in days long past that captives had been marched along this rugged path strewn with boulders and murdered along the route after one particular raid.

One such trapper was captured by the Shawnee and camped beneath its wide canopy one night. As the story goes, his beard was pulled from the roots, and he was burned and branded with pine knots, a scorching piece of wood. After suffering untold agony, he escaped into the wilderness and towards what is now Ash Cave, but not before etching those words into the tree. On moonless nights, the screams of others who did not escape are heard from the valley where the mill once stood, not far from the bridge along the Cedar Falls trail. And, many believe, even during the daylight hours.

Moonville Tunnel
Hope-Moonville Road
McArthur, Ohio 45651
39.307008, -82.321342
Parking: 39.308256, -82.324371

The Darker Side of Moonville

The dark side of Moonville—

There has always been a dark side to Moonville Tunnel. In the old days, it wasn't simply that it was the side farthest from the couple of homes there, and no light penetrated from candles or lanterns sitting near a window past a certain point. Of course, if you asked the train engineers, they would tell you that once they hit that far side of the tunnel after rolling through Hope Furnace, Hope Furnace Station, and Moonville, there was a lengthy stretch of deep, dark forest called Rew Woods and a blackness that never seemed to end until suddenly the twinkle of lights from Ingham or Mineral City came into view. But it was always, too, where the ghostly shenanigans seemed to begin or end depending upon which direction you were heading through that tunnel.

One night in the early 1900s, Ernest Keeton was heading through Mineral City and toward Hope Furnace Station. Just outside Mineral City, and as he walked the tracks, he noticed what he thought was someone wearing a white sheet and walking a stone's throw behind him. The man paused to see if it would catch up, craned his neck to look around and home in on the white sheet, but it stopped too. He began to walk again, once in a while, halting to see if the white sheet was still there. It ceased its steps, too.

Spooked, Ernest began to quicken his pace, finding that the faster he walked, the quicker the white figure walked. The white sheet kept this pace until Ernest realized it had sped up, and it was floating on the opposite end of the ties from him. Yet even though it was directly beside him, it was not making a sound! Ernest was so unnerved that he panicked and began to run. He sprinted past King Station, Ingham Station, Bear Hollow, that long stretch of nothing but deep forest, and all the way to Moonville, with that white thing racing and floating right next to him the entire time. His heart pounded in his chest, and his breath came in ragged gasps. As he sprinted into Moonville Tunnel, it dipped down a ravine into the woods by that dark side of the tunnel. It disappeared, leaving Ernest trembling and alone.

Those who lived in the community shared a common belief that the spirit was a young married woman named Sarah from Mineral City who committed suicide after childbirth in the late 1800s, for Ernest was not alone in witnessing the ghost. Those walking the tracks from Mineral City to Moonville for over a hundred years glimpsed the white apparition following them before it vanished into the dark side of Moonville Tunnel.

On my Moonville night hikes and ghost hunts, folks have seen the white form, too. It is typically near a trestle just outside Ingham Station and by those who linger at the end of the hiking line when returning to the tunnel from Bear Hollow. Maybe you will see it too.

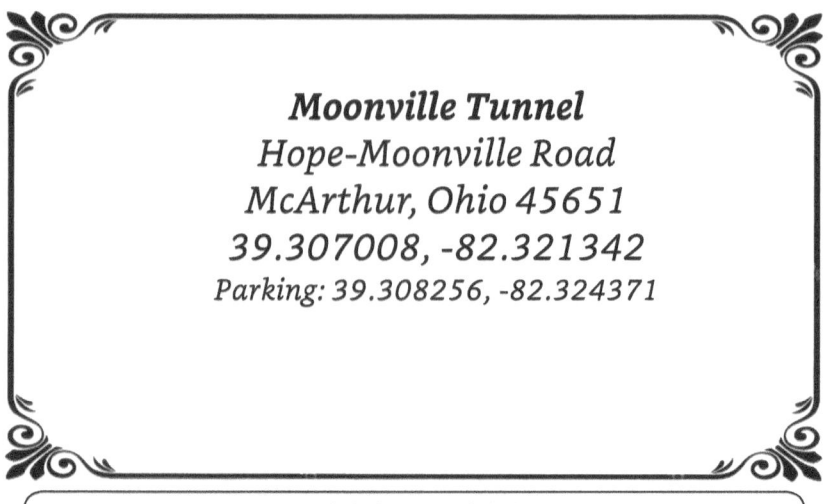

Moonville Tunnel
Hope-Moonville Road
McArthur, Ohio 45651
39.307008, -82.321342
Parking: 39.308256, -82.324371

Rabbit. Rabbit.

Moonville during the ghost hunt.

I have offered night hikes and ghost hunts in the new Vinton County Park, Moonville Tunnel. We've have some really cool paranormal experiences there. One in particular happened recently. All's I can say is "Rabbit, rabbit." Why? Did you know that saying "Rabbit, rabbit" on the first day of the month brings good luck? This belief, steeped in the rich folklore of the Appalachians, traces its roots back to the 1860s. It's said to have been inspired by Lewis Carroll's Alice in Wonderland, where a little girl embarks on an extraordinary adventure after following a rabbit down a hole.

This belief was later echoed in a periodical "Notes and Queries" in March 1909, where a man speaks of his little daughter making a habit on the first day of each month calling up the chimney "Rabbit" as it was believed those who did as their first word of the month, would receive a present. Over the years, this expression was passed along to bring good luck for the rest of the month and, perhaps, a little bit of wealth.

How do I know this? On June 1, I organized one of my usual hikes and ghost hunts in the Moonville Tunnel, known for its eerie atmosphere and paranormal activities. One of the participants had a spirit box. The spirit box is a paranormal research device that scans (in our case, in reverse) through various radio frequencies as "white noise." It is theorized that ghosts and spirits may be able to communicate on different frequencies. He was testing this theory with the equipment and running through a series of questions when he asked, "Do you like hanging around over here?" The answer was quite clear, "I've got more rabbit days-"

When I first heard the ghost's response, I dismissed it as a fluke. But a spark of curiosity led me to do some research. I stumbled upon the "Rabbit rabbit" phrase and discovered that having more "rabbit days" meant the ghost had more good days than bad. The fact that this occurred on the first day of the month made a fascinating connection that added a new layer of intrigue to our ghost-hunting experience. So there you have it, a bit of folklore passed along to us from a ghost. Rabbit, Rabbit.

King Hollow Tunnel/
Mineral Tunnel
Rockcamp Road
New Marshfield, Ohio 45766
Tunnel: 39.321142, -82.280371
Parking: 39.319930, -82.284475

The Eight Foot Ghost of King Hollow Tunnel

King Hollow Tunnel also known as Mineral Tunnel—

When the folks with the Moonville Rail Trail Association tamed back the overgrowth along an old set of railroad tracks near Zaleski, Ohio for a hike, bike, and horse trail, they never expected to also reveal a few ghosts along the way, but they did. This is the story of one of those spirits, the Eight Foot Ghost of King Hollow/Mineral Tunnel.

There's an old train bed deep within the forests of southeastern Ohio, a remote path found by taking buckled pavement streets and sketchy gravel roads. The tracks were built in the 1850s for the Marietta and Cincinnati Railroad.

They passed through coal mining towns like Hope Furnace Station, Moonville, Ingham Station, Kings Station, and Mineral City. As no streets connected the wee town of Moonville Station to the larger community around Mineral City, the 3 1/2 miles of track between the two was a hub of activity for coal miners and their families traveling from one place to another, night and day. They had to cross long wooden trestles high over the shallow waters of Hewett Fork or Raccoon Creek and traverse dark tunnels with no manholes to escape, hoping a train would not come and catch up to them partway through. The level tracks were carved through high hills, so along its path were dangerous cliffs to ascend or descend. Frantic climbing or desperate freefalling were the only way to avoid an oncoming train in the cuts. It was not uncommon for folks to die on those tracks as many used them, and the trains barreled through at tremendous speeds running this remote route. Most believe this is why an unusually high number of spirits are seen and heard there. Much folklore about its supernatural side has been passed down over the last 150 years.

Within the haunted walls of the tunnel—

Paranormal things happen here even today, especially since the Moonville Rail Trail Association forged a new route over the old tracks in recent years, opening up a more easily accessible path for hikers, bikers, and horseback riders.

It isn't unusual for those traveling its passage to experience mysterious connections with the long dead along the isolated three-and-a-half-mile stretch of Moonville Rail Trail between Moonville and Mineral, both night and day. EMF detectors react. Voices and music where long-gone houses once stood are heard. Full-body apparitions even show up once in a while and are caught on camera and video. As if hiking in the dark of night is not enough, we commonly get supernatural interactions when I guide hikers on twilight story-telling, ghost-hunting expeditions. A few have even come face to face with a ghost.

Some of these interactions have yet to be fully explored. Not long ago, most of the old rail bed was lost beneath a hundred years of forest growth when coal mines and the communities around them were abandoned. Now that the passage is open, those passing the old ghost towns can explore their spooky side. One such place is between Ingham Station and Mineral.

A ghost wandered near a particular wooden train tunnel called the Mineral Tunnel or Kings Hollow Tunnel. It was witnessed by many unlucky enough to walk that lonely section of track on a moonless night. It would appear near Mineral City near the tunnel and once in a while around Ingham Station. The spirit was described as a man with brown skin, eight feet tall, appearing to walk on stilts, and wearing a miner's cap with a lamp on its head and the flame flowing over his shoulders. It was known to crawl through the tunnel spider-like and chase the unwary to Ingham Station. The ghost's existence was explained as this:

Twenty-three-year-old Pleasant Dexter "Dex" was a coal miner and a section man for the railroad. He worked in Mineral City and lived with his parents in Ingham Station, about two miles away. Each day, Pleasant took the tracks to work. At night, he headed home along the same isolated route. Sometimes, it was far after dark as he was young, and the young are driven to be wild, restless, and to take risks by nature.

But on May 4, 1927, Pleasant's daily commute would end. He left friends in Mineral City late at night and headed for home at Ingham Station. His path should have taken him a short time as it was just a couple of miles away.

The young man just needed to go through King Hollow Tunnel, past King Station, and to his mama and dad's house. It was a straight route, but slower than usual. He had complained before he left town that his feet were aching, so he removed his shoes and padded along the splintery wooden railroad ties into the darkness in his bare feet.

But sometime during the night, he stopped to rest, lay down on the tracks, and fell asleep. During that time, three trains passed through. A man heading along the tracks discovered his broken and battered body on the west end of King Hollow Tunnel the next day. Shortly after, the ghost began to show—a tall, dark man spider-creeping and crawling around the tunnel and following folks toward Ingham Station as if he was still trying to get home.

But he is also a prankster, I believe! I did a solo ghost hunt from the town of Mineral and through the old King Hollow Tunnel one dark later winter night. I spent several hours within testing equipment from EMF detectors and spirit boxes to thermal cameras and video recorders. It was a quiet night with lots of research and little results—or so I thought. I finally gave into the bitter cold and the ghost's non-cooperation. I packed up my equipment, loaded it into my backpack, and headed on out.

It was not until I returned to my office and my little desk where I delve into my findings, watching hours of videos and ogling pictures over and over to see if there is anything out of the ordinary that I saw the reality. The ghosts were there; I was just not aware.

Several times, in the complete darkness, I had walked from one end of the tunnel to the other, leaving one full-spectrum night video camera on a tripod (with a huge night vision light so I could film in the dark) running while I researched. The tunnel is made of wood covered in creosote to preserve it. It burns the nostrils so my footsteps were quick to the other side as was my return. While I was doing so, I heard little more than Canada Geese squawking at each other in the dark of night in a nearby pond. Yet, upon watching the video, it was quite clear I was not alone. When I walked the tunnel passage each time, the camera would move slightly, followed by the sound of a snicker. Then it would turn off and on several times by unseen hands!

Me, walking into the darkness of the tunnel at night thinking I am alone, but actually surrounded by ghosts—

Then, right before I left, I had turned on the spirit box and told the ghosts I was getting ready to leave because they were not very social tonight. In fact, I was a bit insulted by their distant behavior since I took the time to hike out there. I bid a goodnight, and five separate voices said, "Goodnight, Jannette," five different times.

West State Street Cemetery
West State Street and
Cemetery Street
Athens, Ohio 45701
39.332356, -82.105851

Weeping Angel

In the old West State Street Cemetery, there is a monument dedicated to the memory of the unknown buried in the cemetery since 1804. It was bestowed by the Athens High School in 1924 and has a large angel on a pedestal. Those passing by have seen her weeping, moving, and even fluttering her wings .

One of my jobs as a folklorist and passing along stories for the next generation is to collect narratives or reports from others who may have witnessed tales or lore. Here is one of them:

"OMG that statue of the angel, I don't have the pictures anymore but I took 3 pictures, first one eyes closed, 2, one eyes closed and I decided to provoke it 3 one eyes open, it's still upset me because it made of cement. Some children were walking home from school and I asked one boy 'aren't you scared walking through here?,' he looked me in the eye and said this to me, 'Mister I live in the house right there and if you want to see something, when it's a full moon and it's raining, you can see her wings flapping.' That was back in 2004, haven't been back to Athens Ohio in a long time—"

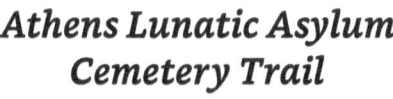

Athens Lunatic Asylum Cemetery Trail
8000 Dairy Lane
Athens, Ohio 45701
39.314654, -82.115208

The Old Asylum Ghosts

The old asylum in Athens—

The old Athens Asylum and its grounds are haunted. Ghosts of its past still walk the floors of the building, amble along the property, and pass through the cemeteries. Some have seen them peeking out the windows as they stand below the old buildings, peering upward. People tell me that they have seen their shadows above the graves. It is not surprising that the location has hosted many ghosts, as it served as a mental health facility from 1874 to 1993, accommodating numerous guests.

I was driving my daughter and two of her friends home from a football game in town some years ago. At the time, you could visit the old asylum grounds after dark. It was a rite of passage for high schoolers to drive a specific brick road leading uphill and passing an asylum cemetery before the lane circled in front of old Building 26, which was touted to once house the criminally insane. There was but one way in and one way out. It was the practice to turn out the lights, making your way slowly around the circle before stopping in front of the building.

One ghost story that stood out among others included the evil spirit of a criminal who would attack the vehicles. He would do all those horrifying things ghosts do to frightened teens in horror films. At the time, this ghost also sported a chainsaw. While he subdued those in the vehicle, the dead arose from the cemetery below to help. They dragged those within the car into the forest beyond. Although we did not know it at the time, we would face this evil entity that very evening.

It was late at night and Halloween time, and I had just passed the main drive leading up to the asylum. A hushed conversation in the back seat of my car became quite heated. I peered into the rearview mirror as I had heard part of the discussion that went something like this— "So just ask her to drive up there. I won't let anything happen to us." The voice was deep, so I recognized it as the boyfriend of my daughter's friend—a high school football player who was still a bit arrogant and high from a winning game that night. I looked into the rearview and saw all three faces with cagey eyes looking at me. "You know I could hear the entire conversation; I'm two feet away in a closed compartment," I piped up. "But, sure, I will drive you up to the asylum." I did not mind. I thought that, indeed, it would be better if an adult drove them up there than the three teens taking an unsupervised trip that might end like one of those horror movies. Since I missed the main entrance, I took a side drive.

As my car crept up the old path, the football player, sitting in the center of the backseat, threw a protective arm around my daughter and then one around her friend and grinned. I heard him cooing to them like he had a semi-automatic weapon tucked into his t-shirt to fight off whatever bad thing was ahead. I admit the drive was creepy.

We rolled the windows down as we passed the main administrative building and then several living quarters. The air in the car grew oppressive as we bumped along the raggedy brick road past the old cemetery. It was silent, too silent. When we reached the peak of the hill, my daughter advised me to turn off the lights, cruise slowly along the road, and, upon reaching a certain point to stop and turn off the car. I did and began to park when I saw something move. "What is that—?" I started, interrupted by a loud grind of a chainsaw. In less time than it took for me to gasp a breath, the car was surrounded by an army of blood-dripping creatures running feverishly with a chainsaw-wielding, wild-eyed beast of a man at their heels.

A scream slipped up from the backseat of my car. I watched as the boy in the backseat, who had only moments earlier been a fearless, seasoned warrior preparing for battle, peeled back his lips in a high-pitched cry and dove to the car floor. He abandoned the two girls, desperately trying to roll up their windows and yelling for me to—"Drive!" I could not drive away as we were surrounded by figures everywhere.

What I did *not* know for probably the most horrifying four minutes of my life was that one of the fraternities had set up a haunted trail for different groups of students. I had taken a little-used backway onto the asylum grounds, and we had happened upon it by accident on both sides. The fraternity thought I was the first car of their reserved groups to get there that night. They got a test drive and we got the scare of our lives. And I believe my daughter's friend stopped dating that boy the next day.

The building was eventually torn down, but that does not stop the other buildings and property in the complex from being haunted. There is a looped trail that hikers can take beginning at the old asylum dairy barn, past the buildings that Ohio University has revitalized for its offices and campus, and through several cemeteries. It is serene and beautiful, and many believe it is haunted, for those who pass through these areas have seen and heard things they can't quite explain. I have too.

*Trail across from
Dairy Barn—*

The Old Cemeteries Trail

I parked at the Dairy Barn and walked across Blackburn Road/Dairy Lane and between the two concrete pillars with a nature trail sign just beyond. I took the wooden steps to the first cemetery where those who donated their bodies to Ohio University were buried. (This is the **blue trail** on maps.) This act would grant them identity and dignity because these are the few with their names on their headstones instead of just numbers to remember them.

First Cemetery—

Next, I walked through the middle of the cemetery to the second cemetery within view. The path is sketchy here, so I hiked to the far right corner, upper hill, where there was a sign for the nature trail (there is another in the central section, but that is the ending point).

Trail End —

Trailhead —

Second cemetery—

I followed the dirt path through the woods and then across a creek past the 'High Ropes Challenge Course,' used by the university in their Outdoor Pursuits Challenge Program. I made a right (you can see the challenge area to the left), and then, where the brick walkway comes up to the left, I made a left (about 0.13 miles). This path took me on the **yellow trail**, which passes the third cemetery after a forest hike.

View of the asylum buildings after turning right and away from the Challenge Course and getting ready to turn on the brick road.

Third cemetery—Note the odd line of graves. These were once in the typical pattern of a circle used in early times around a central monument or flag. But a superstitious volunteer, worried they were being touted as a "witch circle," pulled them from their resting place and misplaced them in rows. Now the bones are mislaid, and probably the reason ghosts have been seen wandering aimlessly there now looking for them!

After the third cemetery, I made a left on Water Tower Road heading toward the Athens University Observatory. The nature trail signs end here. (This is the location of the building where my daughter, her friends, and I had our ghost story.)

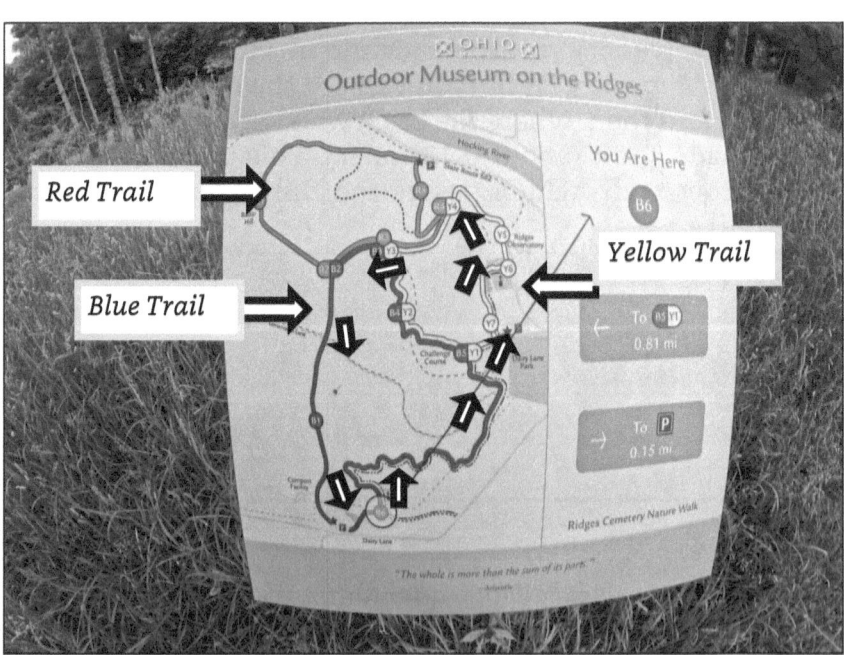

I passed the observatory to my right and continued past the gate along an old service road. This took me through the preserve forest area, old asylum orchards, a modern composting area, and through a small parking area. It is difficult to see, but at the far end of the parking area, to the left, is a small dirt trail that leads along a pond and back to Cemetery 2, where you can cut through back to the Dairy Barn and parking.

When the asylum was young, the property was well-maintained with landscaping features like water fountains. Buildings were found throughout the landscape and nearly hidden in the overgrown patches; you can also see remnants of the past—pieces of dishes, eating utensils, teacups, and foundation stones. Those who walk the trails here have related seeing shadowy figures that follow them curiously, but not in a harmful way. They hear voices that they cannot quite discern are sweeping up from the town below or are of the ghostly type until something is whispered close to their ears.

You can walk around the buildings during daylight hours, and explore the property. Once, a woman at one of the paranormal events I attend approached me to tell me she was doing just that, strolling the grounds and taking pictures of the main old historical building, when she saw someone at a window. Some of the buildings are restored and in use. Believing it was office staff within, she spontaneously waved at the woman. The lady waved back. Then she leaned forward like she would press her forehead to the glass for a better view below. Instead, her face seemed to float partway through the glass to the other outside, and she vanished!

Hope Furnace
Lake Hope State Park
27331 OH-278
McArthur, Ohio 45651
39.331741, -82.340341

Night Watchman

The furnace and the property in earlier days.

In the mid-1800s, there was once a furnace that processed iron ore where Lake Hope State Park now stands. Hundreds of men worked there, timbering the hills for the wood burned to make charcoal to fuel the furnaces, working at the furnace, or hauling the ore.

The furnace and the property today where the buildings once stood.

Little remains but the ruins of the furnace chimney. It is enough, though, to harbor a ghost. Sometime during the twenty years that the furnace made the iron, a night watchman overlooking the furnace fell to his death into the furnace's fiery pit. Almost immediately after, when the bosses would have their meetings in one building on the property, there would be several loud bangs upon the door. When answered, nobody was there.

It was not easy keeping workers during the night watch, too, as a phantom lantern would follow the path of the dead man's last walk through the building and disappear as it came to the pit. Even now, vehicles driving the state route in front of the ruins of the furnace have seen a dim light hovering in mid-air where the building once stood around the chimney. Those walking the path between the parking area and the corpse of the furnace have heard banging raps as if the ghost is still trying to get within the long-gone building!

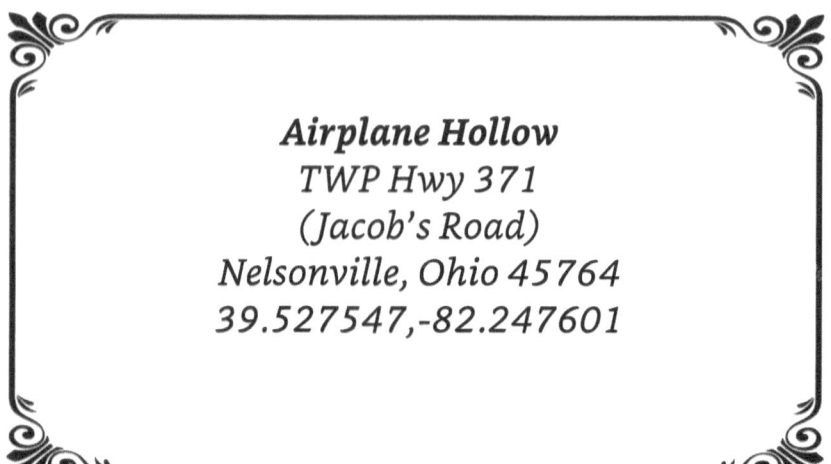

Airplane Hollow
TWP Hwy 371
(Jacob's Road)
Nelsonville, Ohio 45764
39.527547,-82.247601

The Legend of Airplane Hollow: *It Calls Things In and Won't Let Them Out*

Airplane Hollow—

I want to share this story with you of a mysterious and haunting event, which was told to me by some folks whose families have lived in the Carbon Hill/Nelsonville mining communities of southeastern Ohio for well over a hundred and twenty years. The story happened to them, leaving an indelible mark on their lives. This is the legend of Airplane Hollow-

Sometime during the 1970s, the sound of a twin-engine plane circling the town of Nelsonville broke through a violent storm. A couple and their three children living in a modest two-story home about 4 or 5 miles away heard it, as did the wife's grandfather sitting in a recliner in the living room. One by one, all but the grandfather made their way into the kitchen to peer out the window above their sink and into the gloomy night. The engine's roar seemed far above their home before it faded away and then returned. Each time the sound disappeared, they waited for it to return, watching the lightning flash in the sky so perhaps it would shed some light on the mysterious plane. Suddenly, a muffled explosion shook the house, and the hills filled with light. It was silent before they had finished stunned gasps, barring the sounds of the storm.

The mother and father rushed from the room, frantically grabbed jackets and truck keys, and made plans to get help. They had no phone, so they would have to drive down the rutted roads that were, most likely, flooded from the rains to get to the police station. Perhaps others had heard of the plane crash, but maybe they did not. No sirens were ringing out. But before they could cross the living room, the grandfather, still sitting calmly in his chair, stopped them cold in their tracks. "You don't need to go out there in that storm," he said, shaking his head. "It won't matter."

His granddaughter was angered at his callousness and told him so. "It won't matter?" she asked aghast. "But what if nobody else saw it and the people in that plane are still alive? How can you be so mean?"

"They aren't alive," he told her as he shook his head. "They've been dead over thirty years. That plane crashed in the spring of 1941. Put a big rut in the hill when it hit it and took out a bunch of trees. I know. I've seen it. Everybody died inside. But the plane doesn't seem to know that. It keeps coming back every time there's a bad storm around here like it's looking for its dead passengers or something—"

He was right. On May 16th, 1941, the strange sounds of a plane circling over and over outside Nelsonville overrode the roar of gusty winds during a full-blown storm. Some noted that the motor was turning off and on as if the pilot was experiencing engine troubles.

Others witnessed flares tossed to the ground as if those aboard were trying to illuminate the hills below for an emergency landing. The pilot, who had departed Louisville on a flight to Pittsburgh with four other crew members, desperately attempted to find a place to force land in the gale winds. Not long after, there was an explosion as the twin-engine military plane slammed into a hillside outside town, ripping a swatch of trees, brush, and earth 300 feet. It was a military flight, and the pilot of the Beechcraft AT-7 basic combat navigation training plane circled for nearly a half hour, frantically searching for a landing spot in the rough wooded terrain.

The aircraft ripped a 300-foot swatch of trees, brush, and earth on the Peter Dawley farm by a raggedy dirt roadway just a few hundred feet from Fred Christian's house. But some wreckage and the corpses were scattered to the Sol Johnson farm nearby and down a ravine and into the creek. It missed their homes and neighboring farmsteads. But five military men died in the wreck. Roads were barricaded by nearby Camp Nelson Civilian Conservation Corps workers and the state highway patrol from sightseers. A search party frantically combed the hillside in the blackness of night with only the lightning, flashlights, and car lights to find the remains. It took several days to comb through the countryside as the wreckage was scattered all over the road, hollow, swollen creek, and into neighboring hills.

After the grandfather told the couple about the airplane crash long ago, they wanted more from the story than their grandfather had told them that night. The next day, the curious couple went to where they had heard the explosion and thoroughly searched the site. They could only find the deep gouges in the hillside, now nearly overgrown, that the grandfather had talked about and trees still marred from the doomed flight so many years earlier. But they also saw something peculiar, something unnatural in a single, bent shape trudging in short strides along the roadway. They thought it was nothing more than a tree canopy casting an eerie shadow on the muddy road. Yet, when they walked toward it, the shadow disappeared.

The old hollow—

They left quickly because the woman's grandfather had told them about that, too—"You stay away from that place," he said before they left that day. "Nothing good ever came out of that hollow. IT calls things in and won't let them out. There are things up there you don't want to know about. Leave IT be, whatever IT is." They had not asked what those "things" were. Now they knew, and they would never forget.

If you continue along Jacobs Road, there is an intersection where you can turn left to Dawley Cemetery (folks have heard a ghostly babe's cry there) or you continue to the right on the pothole ridden Jacobs Road. After you cross over Sand Run Road, it turns into Burton Hill Road and there is a small pull-off to the right that leads to Tinker's Cave. (39.545617, -82.226326)

Tinker's Cave—

Shep Tinker, a local thief in the mid-1800s, and the horses he was known to steal, haunt this recess cave. Shep disappeared one day, and some believe locals hanged him inside the cave. For years, visitors to the cave have heard groans within along with ghostly horse nickers!

Richland Furnace
Superior Wildlife Area
Wilbur Road
Richland, Ohio
Parking (4 wheel drive):
39.196451,-82.594301

Ghosts in the Old Richland Furnace Ghost Town

Richland Furnace—

Ghost towns tend to be overlooked when folks are searching for spirits. Most of the time, this is because those who lived there and passed along the stories are long gone. I would not be so sure about the latter, as I love to explore old ghost towns, and occasionally, I run into those who once lived there and died there in the past. Take, for instance, Richland Furnace in the Vinton and Jackson County areas of Ohio.

During the 1800s, a specific section called the Hanging Rock Iron Region was a broad belt extending from Logan in Hocking County to Mt. Savage in Carter County, Kentucky. There were 69 furnaces in the region producing iron at one time, and the area became a leading producer. One of these furnaces still stands in the Superior Wildlife Area near Richland Furnace State Forest. A large community was built around this furnace, with many homes and workers from tree cutters (who provided burned wood for charcoal for fuel) to the furnace workers. Little remains of its past but the carcass of the furnace, old foundation stones, and bricks from the school, homes, offices, and old roads that can still be followed. And dead people.

One day, I was hiking along the old road through the community. You must understand that it isn't much of a town anymore. The school is torn down. The homes are gone except for a few root cellars here and there. The road is more like an ATV trail than a street to get to the small parking area; I must drive over several creeks. Then, there is the overgrown road hike to the town proper and furnace. As I walked into the town, I saw someone ambling quickly near the top of the old furnace between the road and where the old schoolhouse once stood. I hollered out, "Hey! How are you doing?" Just to let them know I was there. It was hunting season, and I had my orange vest on, but I was not particularly eager to startle someone with a gun.

I saw the figure moving above me, and whoever it was appeared excited to see me but was busy doing something else. Then I saw a hand come into the air, like a wave. The figure began to descend toward me, making a quick jumping dash along an old path with a steep slope, the kind someone takes when traveling down a hillside fast while trying to avoid rocks. I stood there thinking that they were coming to chat. It was undoubtedly a shorter male wearing a dark shirt and dark pants. I watched him bound, bound, bound down the hill, and then, on the last little section, he appeared to be lifting a knee and both arms as if to take flight as people do before hopping over a long puddle. He leaped. And he vanished before my eyes. I stood there for longer than I should, staring at that empty space between us, turning in a circle twice to make sure I did not miss something because it was so peculiar. Yet, nobody was there.

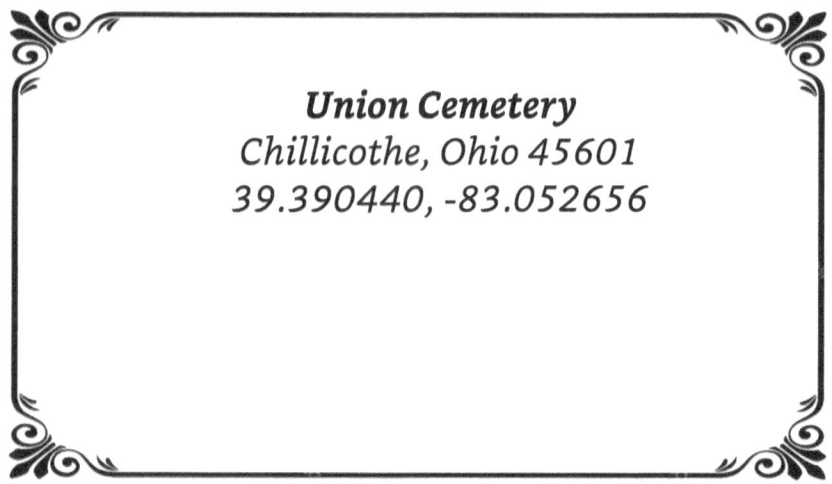

Union Cemetery
Chillicothe, Ohio 45601
39.390440, -83.052656

Elizabeth's Grave

Union Cemetery and Elizabeth's lone grave

When a gravestone began moving on its own accord within a cemetery in a remote section outside Chillicothe, Ohio, travelers once flocked to witness a ghostly form in its wake. This is one of the old legends of Elizabeth's Grave.

The cemetery's location is no longer secluded along the short stretch of Union Lane within Pleasant Valley Wildlife Area, just outside Chillicothe. Once an eerie drive along a far backroad, the forested area has been replaced by new homes almost to the spot where the old Presbyterian Church used to stand, and now, only the Mount Union-Pleasant Valley Cemetery graveyard remains, with broken monuments and even old headstones scrapped in piles in the rear. It appears just another old graveyard lost to time. But this place where the dead were laid to rest is special; it holds much of the prominent McCoy clan, one of the earliest settlers to this part of the country.

Several generations lived, loved, and died on this land. Then, the state gobbled up the property surrounding it for a hunting area and it seemed left to waste; most of the gravestones are now destroyed by vandals and lay strewn about. The area is littered with remnants of hunting season and the curious —beer cans, shotgun shells, and trash from local fast-food restaurants, carelessly thrown out of car windows by patrons. The homesteaders who lived, worshipped, and died here are long gone, but there is one thing, barring the destruction of the once beautiful church and grounds, that remains-a haunting. This old cemetery is home to one of Chillicothe's most enduring legends— Elizabeth's Grave.

For years, those who dare to seek out ghosts have traveled the spooky old gravel, pothole-ridden road, pausing in the drive just outside the cemetery proper, for to pass into the perimeter after dusk would not only bring bad luck but also dispel any signs of a ghost. They sat on the hoods of their cars or by the roadway to wait for a particular mist to slip up from a patch of woods behind the graveyard. On certain nights, the lucky ones would glimpse a white form materialize as if from deep beneath the hallowed earth, a fog that circled and formed into that of a woman. Then, she floated parallel to the woodlot along the overgrown grass and weeds. She passed the location of the old church until she came to a place where old gravestones once stood beneath a majestic old tree. Those who visited called her Elizabeth.

The oldest stories of the haunting explain that the family buried the dead woman's corpse by that church and near that tree well over a hundred years ago, next to her kin. However, an aged oak busted during a windstorm or vandals on a drunken spree toppled the gravestone. Mislaid, the tombstone was later dragged back to its proper position, or maybe the wrong site, by a caretaker unaware of the appropriate place to leave it. Eventually, it was tossed like garbage with others to one far corner. The strange thing was that each time it was hauled away, the headstone returned to that place beneath the tree, where the ghost had returned before fading away. And those whose mortal hands moved it for the pleasure of scaring their friends or more sinister motivations came to horribly bad luck for quite some time, and most until the day they died.

Dillon Falls
Dillon Falls Road
Zanesville, Ohio 43701
39.971727, -82.057721

Ghost of the Old Quaker Burial Ground

The area of Dillon Falls—

When Pennsylvanian Moses Dillon traveled as a companion to a Quaker minister through the Zanesville area toward Coshocton in 1803 as a missionary to the Wyandot, he took a side trip along the Licking River, an early trade route and tributary of the larger Muskingum. The two camped on a grassy spot at a particular section of falls along the river, and Dillon noted the rich coal deposits, the water power that could be used for industry, and the site's beauty.

So drawn to the area, the man sold his farm and returned with his family a few years later, at age 56. He founded a village with a grist mill, trading post, sawmill, forge, and blast furnace where workers made hollow-ware (cast iron tableware and cooking ware like skillets). The hamlet flourished and became Dillon's Falls Village, boasting about 50 families. Just up the road, he set aside a small plot for a burial ground.

The old burial grounds—Dillon Cemetery, Licking Road in Zanesville — 39.948767, -82.027106

The family prospered off this venture for nearly half a century, and Moses Dillon lived to the ripe old age of 92. He died on August 17, 1839. Eventually, the coal ran out, the iron ore in the vicinity was exhausted, and the dam he had built to harness the waters became valueless when another business built a dam along the river. The homes constructed for the workers were eventually moved away, the villagers left, the works fell to ruin, and the place of Moses Dillon's dreams became a ghost town. But in the early 1900s, along with the interurban railway, a town began to grow where the old industries once stood. And the railway built a two-story telegraph station not far from the falls.

During this time, folks realized Moses Dillon may be dead, but his spirit had never left his beloved Dillon Falls Village. His ghostly form strolled from the small Dillon Cemetery along Licking River Road and the railroad tracks and back to the vicinity of the old blast furnace, where the telegraph station then stood. Sometimes, he would float upward and peer through the second-story window of the telegraph station and spook the operator within.

Driving the path where Dillon's ghost walked—

You can drive from the Old Quaker Burying Ground, aka Dillon Cemetery, along Licking River Road and stop to view the falls at Dillon Falls Community Fire Station Township Park. It is near Zanesville. You may also glimpse old Moses Dillon, trudging along the aged road with back bent and eyes fixed on the route ahead, still drawn to the falls.

Southwest Ohio

John Rankin House
6152 Rankin Hill Road
Ripley, Ohio 45167
38.751049, -83.842605

Ghostly Steps toward Freedom

The last steps to Rankin House.

A house sits atop a lonesome grassy hill overlooking the Ohio River in Ripley. It is neither large nor majestic, just a simple square brick dwelling with unadorned windows and bare wooden front and back doors. Along the steep and forested hillside leading up to the home from the town below are a series of lopsided wooden and stone steps overgrown with grasses and small tree saplings. To either side of the old walkway is a long set of walls made of gray stone, about three feet in height, and sitting slightly akilter.

The stone walkway climbs so precipitously and steeply upward that just looking at it warrants stopping to catch one's breath. It would appear insignificant to most. It is not. Thousands used these very steps during the darkest hours of the night, strangers desperately seeking refuge and running for their lives. They were the enslaved escaping from the South, and John Rankin, a Presbyterian minister, built the house at the site so the steps could be used often by those who sought his help and freedom. A light in a window meant it was safe for the runners to approach. Once within, family members secreted the runners in an attic or a cellar beneath a barn. Ohio was a free state, but federal law required that the fugitive slaves be apprehended and returned. So even though they had crossed the river, their safety and the safety of those who harbored them, who could be jailed for coming to their aid, was at risk.

Sometimes, visitors walking the path up those stairs have been approached by someone from its past. As their feet follow the trail of hundreds of escaped slaves, they hear the frantic patter of footsteps behind them. When they turn to see who is approaching, nobody is there.

Cincinnati Music Hall
1241 Elm Street
Cincinnati, Ohio 45202

The Dead Don't Rest

Cincinnati Music Hall

Those who visit Music Hall, home of the Cincinnati Opera and Cincinnati Symphony Orchestra, have periodically witnessed ghostly figures appear and disappear. Their presence is explained like this: In the late 1870s, the city built a red-brick convention center along the Miami Canal, where once an orphan asylum, hospital, pest house, and potters field stood. This industrial exhibitions building was designed for musical arts performances in a central location and north and south exposition wings. One was for mechanical machinery and the other for horticulture.

During the initial construction, crowds gathered as workers turned the dirt over and dug up the rotting corpses of the potter's field, dead buried there. Then, people began collecting souvenirs of the bones and effects lying within, some medical students even returning after police dispersed the pilfering vandals to collect skulls for their classroom.

However, only when the site was excavated for an elevator at an exposition hall, did people begin witnessing ghosts. Workers came across bones, and without a better place to dispose of them, the men placed them in a barrel, tapped on a lid, and stored them in some dark recess of the building. A night watchman, slightly annoyed by the noises caused by the rambling ghosts after that, frequently found himself chasing groans and moans. Often, footsteps, some soft and some cumbersome, would follow his movements. When he walked, the steps would follow. When he stopped, the ghostly strides would pause, too. The watchman heard whispers and soft chatters, but making haste to the location of the mysterious voices and holding a lantern aloft left no solution to where the source of the noises could be found.

These phantom-like appearances were intensified by fog and rain. They appeared to diminish when large audiences attended a musical performance. Although they never appeared in visible form to this particular watchman, people visiting the expositions saw with their own eyes a pale woman with long flowing hair in the garb of much earlier years floating along the floor. When they approached her, she faded away until there was nothing but a haze before them. Some suppose these dead have been abruptly awakened from the grave, perhaps confused or angry and looking to put their bones back together.

Five Rivers Metroparks
Island Metropark
Bessie Little Bridge
Parking: 101 E Helena Street
Dayton, Ohio 45404
Bridge:
39.782727, -84.202783

The Ghost of Bessie Little Bridge

Bessie Little Bridge—

A bridge on Ridge Avenue in Dayton crosses over the peaceful waters of the Stillwater River. Hikers enjoying a walk along the Stillwater River Recreation Trail and travelers along the roadway have for years seen a young woman pacing about on the bridge before she vanishes. The curious race to investigate, believing a young woman has jumped to her death into the waters below. But the Stillwater River surface remains calm. No body is found, and no one has yet to stop the young woman from disappearing into the murky waters. She is a ghost, and her story goes like this—

On September 2, 1896, Dayton was amid a late summer heat wave. One young Cincinnati man, E.L. Harper, visiting relatives in Riverdale, went to the river to cool off with a swim. As he undressed and eased partway into the water, Harper noted a shoe bobbing lazily toward the surface with a twig seemingly stuck within. Curious, he floated over only to discover that the shoe was not attached to a stick but instead the decaying limb of a woman whose body was bloated and grossly discolored. Shaken, Harper dressed and made haste to the nearest boathouse, hailing those within who called for the police and rowed out to the body, towing it to shore, awaiting the authorities to arrive.

Dr. Lee Corbin was the coroner then, and after a quick look-see of the deceased, he found no signs of mischief. While word spread throughout the neighborhood, newspaper reporters began to pour into the area seeking information. Corbin hastily deemed the death a drowning or suicide and sent the unidentified woman's remains to the undertaker. Dayton Police Chief T.J. Farrell also brought in Assistant Police Surgeon Fred Weaver, whose job entailed investigating unexpected deaths at crime scenes. Weaver performed a brief autopsy, found no marks of violence, but discovered the dead woman had been pregnant for several months. Due to the decomposition, Weaver had her buried quite quickly.

An article about the unidentified body was printed in newspapers—that of a woman between the ages of 25 and 30, with a high forehead, pug nose, and a wide mouth. Her dark brown hair was held up with distinctly designed celluloid pins. Upon hearing of the investigation, three teen boys visited Chief Farrell's office, stating that they had been fishing on the early Friday morning and had found little pools of blood on the Y.M.C.A. Athletic Field bridge and railing, along with wagon marks and two tortoiseshell hair combs adorned with baubles and laying in a puddle of blood. They had pocketed the hair combs, thinking just a fight had occurred, until they heard of the missing woman, then handed the combs over to Chief Farrell. Within days, a cashier at the local Cooper Hotel was reading a newspaper and recognized the description of the mysterious dead woman as a previous boarder.

The worker called the authorities with the information, and Chief Farrell contacted the woman's mother, Eliza Little. She confirmed by the description and the custom-made celluloid hair combs that the dead woman was her 23-year-old adopted daughter, Bessie. The wayward daughter was forced to leave the family home weeks earlier after Eliza caught Bessie and her boyfriend, 20-year-old Albert Frantz, in a less-than-discreet romantic affair.

The community began to take great interest in the story. Chief Farrell found through Bessie's most recent landlady, Missus Freese, that Bessie left the boarding house at South Jefferson Street on August 27 in quite a rush at 6:10 in the evening, citing that she was late and heading to meet Albert at Boulevard Park near Fifth Street. After that date, she had not returned.

When Frantz was confronted, he told authorities Bessie had been glum as of late because her adopted mother, who disliked him, had caught them together. Bessie had moved away from home, appeared melancholy, and may have tried to kill herself. Curiously, not long after, the Frantz family barn burned up along with Albert's poor horse and buggy. As tiny bits and pieces of evidence began to surface, they interlocked neatly together as if to form a jigsaw puzzle. Such not unconvinced that the young woman's death was suicide, Police Chief Farrell had Police Surgeon Fred Weaver perform a more detailed autopsy. Sure enough, there were two revolver holes found in Bessie's skull. It appeared as if Albert had shot Bessie in the head and then burned the carriage to cover up the blood within. Later, a local store clerk declared Albert Frantz had purchased a .32 caliber revolver from him two weeks before the killing. The puzzle was solved! Albert Frantz was arrested for the murder and continued denying his part in her death, stating that Bessie killed herself. During the court proceeding, authorities brought Bessie's head into the courtroom to show that the first shot alone would have killed her. It was completely unheard of that she could have shot herself twice.

Albert Frantz was found guilty at the trial and was electrocuted for his crime. Years later, the Ridge Avenue Bridge over the Stillwater was rebuilt, but old-timers will always remember this bridge as the "Bessie Little Bridge."

Life continued for most in Dayton except for the poor young woman who was murdered and dumped off the bridge into the waters below. Her body was buried at Woodland Cemetery, but her soul was not laid to rest. Because Bessie Little's spirit still walks that bridge.

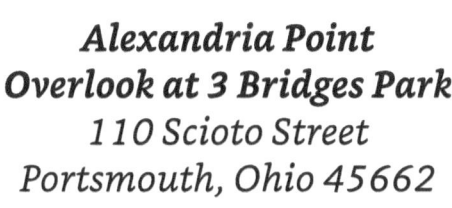

Alexandria Point
Overlook at 3 Bridges Park
110 Scioto Street
Portsmouth, Ohio 45662
38.731315, -83.011224

White Lady Point

A great place to view White Lady Point—

The Kanawha Gal, a paddle wheeler along the Ohio River, was forced to dock on the Kentucky side of the river near Portsmouth one night in the 1800s during a heavy fog. As the boat settled in, a woman standing with a child on a high hilltop on the Ohio side of the river in a white dress caught the crew's attention. She was screaming hysterically and waving her arms frantically.

They could do little in the heavy fog, so the men waited until morning when it slowly parted along the Ohio, haunted all night by shrill cries. When the fog finally lifted, they made their way to the far side of the river and came upon a most unpleasant discovery—a cabin deep in the woods with droplets of blood running from the front door and within, the drag marks of a body leading to a back room. Upon the front door was a bloody handprint, huge in size, larger than any the men could imagine. Yet within, they found nothing more. The crew searched the area. Before long, they came upon a hunter. The shaken man had happed upon the mangled body of a murdered woman in the woods.

They later discovered her name was Mary Fisk, and she had been alone in the cabin with her six-year-old son while her husband was hunting. Sometime during the previous night, a huge and hulking man had entered the home and murdered poor Mary. Search parties never found her son.

Not long after the discovery, passengers and crews on boats floating down the Ohio River and at the mouth of the Scioto River would hear shrill cries from a high cliff that was once a part of an early settlement, the village of Alexandria. Then, they saw a lady in white with mouth gaping wide and arms extended pleading for help when they looked above. Yet, when boat captains sent rescue parties to find her, they came upon nothing but the skeletal remains of an old cabin in the woods with nobody around.

Richardson Forest Preserve
4000 W Kemper Road
Cincinnati, Ohio 45251

Lick Road—The Legend of Amy

Lick Road—

Lick Road winds its way through farmland, then makes a dead-end at Hamilton County Park District's Richardson Forest Preserve. A mysterious legend surrounds this isolated cul-de-sac and the path along Banklick Creek, leading to a bridge. It centers around a girl named Amy, murdered by her boyfriend then dumped into the creek. Her ghostly form winds its way down the path. If you park at the end of the road and honk three times, she appears. If you sit in your car, condensation will form on the windshield with the words HELP ME written in the misty film.

***Darby-Lee Historic
Cemetery***
*5999 Bender Road
Cincinnati, Ohio 45233
Cemetery:
39.099702, -84.653789*

The Legend of the Fiddler Green

Darby-Lee Cemetery—

Darby-Lee Cemetery lies in the woodland overlooking the Ohio River in Delhi Township of Cincinnati. On certain nights, a green light floats along the tombstones at this aged little graveyard. The eerie sound of fiddle rolls along the green grass, nearly hiding the graves before the tune wafts on past toward the river. It is small and protected by an old wooden fence. It has about seventeen ancient gravestones surrounding a pale, aged obelisk in the middle.

This center monument, grayed with age, belongs to the landowner Henry Darby, an avid abolitionist. During the early 1800s, Mister Darby would walk to the tall hill overlooking the Ohio River below, light his lantern, and play his fiddle to signal safety to the escaping slaves crossing over the river from Kentucky. Not long after his death and burial, at the very place he summoned so many to safety, people began to see the glow of his lantern bobbing around the cemetery. They would hear the ghostly, shrill sounds of his fiddle sweeping between the hills and down to the river, still beckoning those below it was safe to cross.

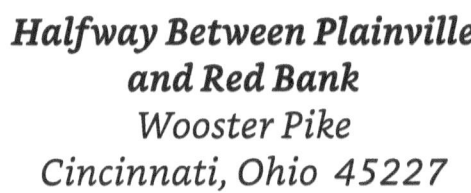

*Halfway Between Plainville
and Red Bank*
Wooster Pike
Cincinnati, Ohio 45227

The Ghost of Newell's Hollow

*Along Newell's
Hollow—*

In the area of Terrace Park, there was once a wooden stockade with 17 cabins and a mill. It was called Covalt's Station, and farmers from all around would risk their lives taking their grain there to have it ground to flour as Shawnee were regularly waiting in the brush for settlers to pass. In the lonely places between forts, settlers were easy to ambush and steal horses and hogs or waylay and murder out of spite.

In September of 1791, James Newell, a resident of Columbia (near the river and Cincinnati Airport-Lunkin Field), was heading to Covalt's Station with a sack of corn. The path he traveled was little more than a trail that follows the same course as Wooster Pike today. Halfway between the settlements, Newell came upon two of his neighbors returning from the mill, Aaron Mercer and Ignatius Ross, who warned the man that they had seen signs of Shawnee up the river. Therefore, the farmer should postpone his trip for another time and turn back. Newell shrugged and told them he would be fine. He already had come this far, and turning around would be a waste of time. Such, he ignored their advice and continued onward.

However, it was almost immediately after the men parted ways that Mercer and Ross heard rifle shots in the direction Newell had taken. They waited a short time to see if there was more gunfire, then sped in the direction of the noise. Along the side of the trail, they came upon Newell nearly dead. A Shawnee hiding behind a tree had shot him. It had only taken one blast and the killer bolted after firing the gun. The men took the dead farmer back to Columbia for burial.

The dark, wooded place where he died was about halfway between Redbank and Plainville and near a small ravine crossing Wooster Pike. After the ambush, this little piece of land became known as Newell's Hollow. On moonless nights, settlers and later townspeople of Plainville talked of James Newell's ghost walking this path, still carrying his sack of corn. Once in a while, those in the vicinity would hear his screams and wails.

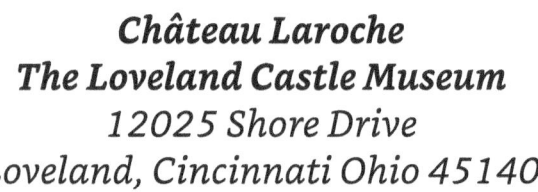

Château Laroche
The Loveland Castle Museum
12025 Shore Drive
Loveland, Cincinnati Ohio 45140

Loveland Castle

Loveland Castle—

In the late 1920s, teacher and news reporter Harry Andrews began to build a castle in what was once a remote area on the banks of the Little Miami River in Loveland. It was specifically intended for a group of boys from his Sunday school class who shared his love of the outdoors, and he called Knights of the Golden Trail. He named the castle Château de la Roche. It started with stones, then empty milk cartons filled with concrete until a huge citadel lay across his land by the 1960s.

As any castle has some romantic joy or tragedy to play out, the latter was in Andrews' past. When he was a medic in World War I, during an epidemic, he contracted cerebrospinal meningitis and was pronounced dead and taken to the morgue. However, he was very much alive but unable to speak or move. A doctor, on a whim, decided to inject Andrews with a new drug called adrenalin, punched his chest, and his heart began to beat again. Six long months later, when news reached home that he was very much alive, his fiancé had already married another man. Mister Andrews remained a bachelor. He spent his life at the castle until he passed away at 91 in April 1981 from injuries sustained after his polyester pants caught on fire trying to stomp out flames while burning trash on the castle grounds.

I remember visiting the castle often when I was young. My dad was the Faith Community United Methodist Church minister in West Chester, who loved taking the youth groups to the Château de la Roche for field trips. Harry Andrews, by then, a gray-haired, gaunt man with an occasional smile, would greet us, give us a tour of his castle, and tell us about his knights for whom he built the castle.

He would then whip out an empty milk carton to display what he used (almost 32,000 of these quart milk cartons) to fill with concrete to make the bricks that created the castle. Before we left, we carried some treats and bags full of empty paper milk cartons we had collected to "pay" for our tour.

It is not surprising to hear Harry Andrews still ambles around his old domain, flitting about as a shadow just out of sight. Some have even seen him staring down at them from a turret before vanishing. I clearly remember he had an offbeat sense of humor with jokes that my dad would laugh at, but we kids would stare blankly like kids do when adults have a funny story that makes no sense. Mister Andrews seemed to think that was even funnier and always grinned. So I imagine he grins now, too, enjoying this life after death and playing gentle pranks on folks who visit.

Old Lafferty Road and Chicken Hollow Road
Ripley, Ohio 45167

Calico Lady of Chicken Hollow

The road to Calico Lady's house—

There are many names for a group of cats—a *dout*, a *clutter*, or a *glaring*. If they are wild or feral cats, they have been called, for a good reason, a *destruction*. But the name for a party of three or more cats that sticks out best in my mind is *clowder*, which comes from the 1700s Middle English term clodder meaning to coagulate or clot like, well, a "clotted mass."

There was once a clowder of cats along old Lafferty Road in Brown County. They belonged to an old woman in a huge and decaying old house along a dark and nearly forgotten road that ran beside a rocky, brush-stubbled creek. As everybody else in her family had long passed, she was alone barring these old strays, and she treated them as if they were her children. They followed her around as such, weaving in and out of her ankles as she strode around inside and outside the home performing daily tasks.

When neighbors passed by on the rutted dirt path in front of her house to get from here to there, the old woman would burst from the door with her shin-length cotton calico dress blowing in the breeze. She would scream and holler to slow down, so they did not hit one of her children. In her clasped fingers, she would always have a dinged-up tin bucket she used to keep scraps of food within to feed her many cats. It dangled there, and she banged it furiously with an old spoon to catch the attention of those inside the buggies and later, cars and trucks. Rumors always prevailed that she was missing two fingers of this very hand because when she fed her nearly feral cats, they would fight amongst themselves to get to the best piece. Often, in their eagerness, they would snap at her fingers holding a tender morsel of food. Occasionally, the bite would cut deep and bring blood.

As she made her way along her overgrown yard in pursuit of those speeding past, around her swarmed her clowder of cats, a lumpy glob of *moggies*, which are mixed breed mutt cats. There were orange tabbies blended with Siamese and Persian or who-knows-what to make a calico mix of oranges and grays, browns and whites. She would scream curses at those passersby, her yowls joining with her cats' caterwauls to slow down their buggy or car as they just might hit one of her tabbies. She was known to jog behind the vehicle for quite a long time.

The old woman died. Most think she tripped over one of her cats. After a while, when neighbors noticed that she did not show up chasing cars, someone brave enough to do so went inside the ancient house and discovered her remains, mostly bones because, well, she was not around to feed the cats, and they had nothing to eat but the old woman.

When they had made a fine feast of her, and there was nothing left, the cats scattered into the forest or died. There was little remaining of the old lady and her kitties but a gooey mix of clotted dried blood and desiccated skin and the woman's old tin bucket still held tightly in her skeletal hand. And there were also lots of orange and white mummified moggy cat remains.

Eventually, the house fell to ruins. After, there were rumors that the old woman's ghost frequently floated from the old home's remains and out into the yard. At her feet, the ghostly cat meows blended with her wails before she vanished. Stories into the 1970s recounted harrowing tales of thrill-seekers taking the rugged Lafferty Road off Chicken Hollow that ran alongside a creek called Lafferty Run to visit the home's remains. When it was still a dirt road, that is, and not a muddy trail. It was a dare. The driver stopped the car. One of the passengers had to get out, close the door behind them, and walk a raggedy trail ridden with creeks and rocks and hills and what remained of old Lafferty Road. They had to find the house and call out for Calico Lady.

Even if she was not nearby, there were still cats hanging around. Cats were running, and cats were lounging on the porch, meowing. Sometimes, no one came. Finally, braver ones walked to the entryway, knocked at the door, called her name again. Calico Lady! That was when she came, Calico Lady, the phantom of an old woman dressed in multicolored clothing and carrying a bucket in her three-fingered hand while the clowder of cats scattered with yowls and meows. And she got mad, really mad, and chased the ghost hunters away. Ghost or reclusive old lady, it did not matter. She scared many over the years.

Now the house is long gone. An old stone foundation remains, riddled with rusty nails, broken bricks from a chimney, and cream-colored creek stones. It is along the nearly dead Lafferty Road, a trail only a little bigger than the width of holding the arms out to the side. It ends in a field. The road is impassible to vehicles, barely on foot. The bridges once running over Lafferty Run are crushed and buried beneath thick stone. Fence designating private property runs on both sides, warning trespassers to stay between the lines.

The remains of the old home—upon my return once when it was less overgrown and still an old road, I heard cat meows. I tried to find the little kitty, more concerned it was lost from a nearby home. After calling and searching for quite some time, I gave up feeling I might be getting tricked by a ghost cat as it never materialized!

But Calico Lady is still there, tucked in the dead arms of the building and the briar-ridden field. Some say she still paces around the old roadway along Lafferty Run, where the path stops right about Chicken Hollow. Back and forth, back and forth, Calico Lady trudges with a crowd of cats yowling at her feet, banging her pan. She yells with her ghostly fist in the air at those who drive slowly past and call out her name.

Dead Mans Hollow
Grave Site
Forest Road 2
Nile Township, Ohio 45684
38.698616, -83.237139

Dead Man Hollow

The hollow and lone grave where a peddler was murdered—

A mysterious grave lies deep within a hollow about nineteen miles from Portsmouth. It is in an area of dense, dark woodland and in a secluded pocket of Shawnee State Forest, surrounded by a winding dirt and graveled roadway. The story of the grave goes like this—

In the 1930s, the Civilian Conservation Corps (CCC) was a federal program that offered jobs to young men to battle high unemployment during the Great Depression. The work was in parks and forestland and designed to open up these natural areas for public recreation. One of these sites where a CCC camp was set up was Shawnee State Forest. At the time, it was nearly inaccessible to the public, so among the jobs of the CCC were building bridges, trails, and roads.

One day, while the men were working on the forest roadway, they found a man's skeletal remains. Wedged within the crevice of a small rock overhang nearby were combs, implements, and tin plates—the type of things a peddler would sell. The bones were later moved and reburied adjacent to the little cleft in the rocks. A stone was set along the right fork of Twin Creek in the hollow to commemorate the peddler. It read: "H. T. Aug. 13, 1824. A. D. Dead M."

Along the old road where the CCC men were working and found the bones. Center, is the grave.

Upon finding the bones, old folks recalled a peddler who, in the 1820s, routinely visited the rural towns nearby and who had oddly ceased calling on farms on his usual route. They remembered hearing that a peddler had paused in the village of Buena Vista in Scioto County along the Ohio River.

After selling his wares, he was directed along a 6-hour rugged footpath northeast to the settlement of Upper Turkey Creek, a community about three miles north of the town of Friendship. He never got to his destination.

Most believed the peddler was ambushed and murdered, but no one knew the truth about how he died, or at least they would not tell. For many years, locals avoided the area of the hollow after dark, reporting ghostly screams, whistling, and strange noises. I have heard them, too. Years ago, I and several others performed a ghost hunt there for a women's retreat at the state park. While we were packing up, a feral cry swept up through the ground at the spot where the old peddler was buried. It was neither coyote, fox, or bobcat. Standing next to a park naturalist, I looked at her.

"Did you hear that?" I asked after a good three seconds of doubt.

"I did." Her face was as pale as a sheet, like my own.

Then, ten years later, during another public ghost hunt, a young boy asked, with a recorder in his hand and referring to the peddler, "Are you here?" It was not the peddler's ghost that answered, but a child's voice instead, "We don't belong here." It was the exact spot where I had found a tiny antique marble the day before.

Dead Man Hollow got its name placed on the map after CCC began its project in 1933 making Shawnee accessible to the public building roads and upon the discovery of bones on the old Taylor property. From 1823-1824, there was a high mortality rate in Portsmouth from "ague" or malaria.

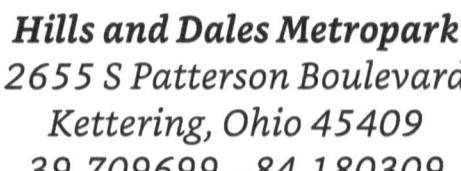

Hills and Dales Metropark
2655 S Patterson Boulevard
Kettering, Ohio 45409
39.709699, -84.180309

Frankenstein's Castle

The Hills and Dales Metropark old stone observation tower, now known as Frankenstein's Castle.

I was collecting some haunted Ohio hiking stories. I stopped at Bloody Bridge near Wapakoneta, Bessie Little Bridge in Dayton, and Caesar Creek State Park outside Waynesville. On a whim, I stopped at "Frankenstein's Castle" (Witch's Tower or Patterson's Castle) near Kettering.

Initially built by boys from the National Youth Administration in the early 1940s as a stone observation tower for the Community Golf Course. The turret-like building was constructed with a stone spiral staircase to an observation deck at the top.

It has been rumored to be haunted, and the story behind the legend is based on an actual event occurring many years ago. On June 14, 1967, 16-year-old Bellbrook High School sophomore Peggy Harmeson and a friend, Ron, had walked to the tower and found shelter within its walls during a thunderstorm. At some point, near the front iron gate, the building was struck by lightning as they leaned against the walls with wet clothing. The two were electrocuted. Ron survived. But Peggy died of severe burns, and rumors were passed that her burnt image remained on step 11, where she had been killed, and sometimes before a storm, ghostly shadows appear. Eventually, the doors had to be sealed with concrete, and the windows were barred to stop the many legend trippers from visiting at night. Nowadays, some say on quiet days at the Hills and Dales MetroPark, where this stone tower is located along a trail, hikers passing by the old stone tower can hear whispers and even muffled screams.

Denver, Ohio
Near Chillicothe

The Ella Light

Near Chillicothe, outside Denver, a light would appear in a wooded area along a dirt road where an old recluse named Cave once lived in a shanty shack with his daughter, Ella. Ella married a man named McDaniels, but her husband soon died. After his death, the father and daughter did not get along well, and their constant screams and yells at each other were heard by neighbors quite often.

Occasionally, Ella would run through the woods screeching and clawing at the air inconsolable as if she had gone mad. One day, Ella vanished, and although an investigation was made, no sign of her could be found; many believed her father had murdered her. Years later, her father died. It was then the light began to materialize, as most believed that the woman's murder could now never be avenged.

Bridge Over Ohio Brush Creek
Dunkinsville, Ohio 45660

The Strange Demise of Julia Eichel

The old bridge over Ohio Brush Creek—

There was not much mention of the young servant Julia Eichel's demise except that she had disappeared mysteriously one winter's night with snow two inches deep upon the ground. She bade her employer, a merchant in Dunkinsville, goodnight and retired to her room. When the family awakened the following day, and the girl had yet to rise to tend to her tasks, someone checked her room, and only the girl's shoes and hat were discovered as if she had just laid them there to sleep. Julia had vanished without a trace; not even footprints were found around the yard.

But Julia's ghost returned over the years, haunting an iron bridge over Brush Creek. Her phantom would appear as clearly as anyone living: a medium-sized woman in black. But what catches the eye is that her feet are bare when she passes close by, and her body has no coat or shawl. Her long black hair streams down her back, and a pale hand hides her even paler face. She glides past without a sound across the bridge and disappears.

Great Miami River Recreational Trail
Middletown, Ohio 45044
39.516801, -84.410266

Ghost Among the Corpses

Near the old cemetery where a ghost would glide—

Middletown was once home to a ghost in an abandoned cemetery. The locals, accustomed to the sight of bits of corpses and skeletons washed along the river banks after a good rain, were taken aback when the ghosts made their appearance. Missus Storms was among the first to report the sighting in March of 1893, a time when others were too anxious to be labeled as overly superstitious. The ghost appeared to her as a massive dark horse that glided over the shoreline as if sprouting wings before disappearing into a mist.

This sighting sparked a wave of similar accounts, with others admitting to seeing the strange creature and even adding that it emitted a deep moan of anguish when it appeared to them. The Great Miami River flood of 1903 washed away most of the cemetery's remains. However, a monument marks its former location along the Great Miami Recreation Trail near the Central Avenue bridge. Or, perhaps, if you are looking for the old city of the dead, watch for the ghostly horse.

Ghost Hollow
Along Eagle Creek in Adams County

A Place Called Ghost Hollow

Eagle Creek passing Ghost Hollow—

In the 1800s in Adams County near Eagle Creek, a common hunting technique was to assemble a group in a line on one end of a field or woods that would make noise (beaters) while moving toward another group of hunters on the other side to frighten their prey into the trap of hunters who would shoot them. It was called a drive. In 1878, a fox drive was advertised, and ten foxes were caught between the beaters and hunters. A local character named Joe Woods came with hounds that broke the ring and chased the foxes away. Neither the foxes nor the dogs were seen again.

A fight ensued, and the hunters were so enraged that they attacked Joe and secured him by chain to a stump. He was forgotten and left to get away on his own. Years would pass, and people in the vicinity of the hunt began to hear groaning sounds along an old ravine. Soon after, a ghost dragging a log and chain appeared before them, followed by a pack of baying hounds. They named the place Ghost Hollow, and it remains so even to this day.

Mid- Ohio

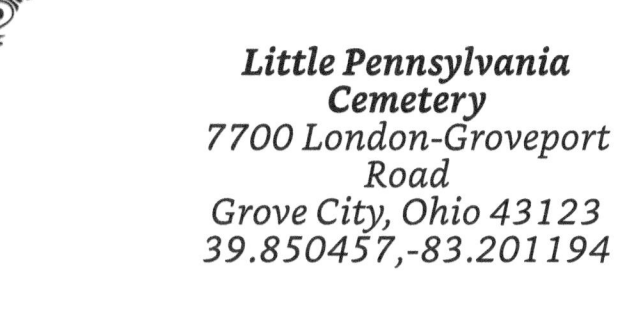

Little Pennsylvania Cemetery
7700 London-Groveport Road
Grove City, Ohio 43123
39.850457,-83.201194

About Wooly Booger Cemetery (or whatever it is called)

Standing in front of Willy's grave—

Big Darby Creek runs 84 miles, and along its route, it passes through the town of Darbydale. Just outside Darbydale is Little Pennsylvania Cemetery. Over the years, it has gained the name of Woolly Booger Cemetery. Some believe it is because a Bigfoot-like creature called a Woolly Booger lurks beneath the shadows of the trees. Others have been told a man butchered his family before killing himself, only to return from the grave as a boogeyman.

Several called this revenant Wooly Booger (or woolly bugger, wooly burger, or . .) and he tries to hurt anyone entering his family plot. There were even a few who believed the murdering beast's name was Willie Butcher because somebody found a headstone belonging to Willie Boucher and when passed along by word of mouth, the name went from Boucher to Butcher and then you got "Willie Butcher" and later, Woolly Booger. The latter has one problem, Willie was only a one-year-old when he died.

Still, there might have been a boogeyman nearby. In 1957, the half-clothed corpse of a young woman was found on a lover's lane road by Big Darby Creek near Darbydale by four teens heading out to fly fish. The murderer had wrapped a bedspread around the body before stuffing it into a raggedy feed sack and dumping it. Police had a tough time finding out who murdered the girl, and many-a-parent probably warned their children from Columbus, past Darbydale, and beyond that they better be in by dark because there was a boogeyman on the loose near Darbydale. They were right. And perhaps . . . he still is.

Otterbein United Methodist Church Cemetery
County Road 62/ Otterbein Road NW
Rushville, Ohio 43150
39.77194, -82.36333

Bloody Horseshoe Grave

This cemetery holds a mysterious grave.

James Kennedy Henry was a farmer near Rushville. When he was 30-years-old in 1844, he decided it was time to settle down and find a wife. Two women caught his eye— Mary Angle and Rachael Hodge. Both were pretty and charming, and James was so smitten with both, he could not decide which one to marry.

One night while heading home from visiting his sweethearts, he fell to sleep on the saddle of his horse. When he awakened, the horse was standing outside the door of Mary Angle. James took it as a sign—fate had decided Mary would be his bride. The two were married on a chilly day in January 1844. It was a tradition for the parents of the bride and groom to give them a gift they could use in their new life as a couple. The newlyweds received one handsome workhorse from Mary's parents and one workhorse from James' parents, so the two had a team of horses to start a farm.

Mary and James were happy together for a little more than a year until Mary died while giving birth to a child. In February of 1845, James buried her in a corner plot at the local Otterbein Cemetery. Distraught, the widowed man would do everything he could to forget Mary—throwing himself into his farming trying desperately to rebuild his life. But there was one thing James did not do. He did not return the horse Mary's parents had given the couple on their wedding day.

James buried Mary in a grave at Otterbein United Methodist Church cemetery.

James took nearly three years before he would begin courting his earlier sweetheart, Rachael Hodge. During this time, in the surrounding area, some whispered that James had broken tradition by not returning the horse to Mary's parents after she died. Mary's family was having a difficult time making ends meet and needed the horse for their farm. There were hard feelings between the families not spoken aloud.

Rachael was only 22-years-old when she took James' hand in marriage. All would seem perfect except for one small thing occurring when James visited his first wife's grave not long after taking his new bride. On the back of Mary's headstone, there was a bloody red shape of a horseshoe! It was an omen that would linger in the back of his mind for many years. James and Rachael had four daughters and were married for nearly eleven years. The couple was happy, but the dark cloud of the horseshoe grave followed James wherever he went.

The bloody horseshoe showed up on this grave.

Then the inevitable happened. The curse would come full swing. While working in the barn one Friday evening, he was kicked in the head by a horse and instantly killed. It was the very horse James had not returned to Mary's parents that put him in the grave. To this day, the bloody horseshoe print is still marking the headstone. Visitors to the cemetery have seen lights and even heard the sound of horses roaming around the graves. Yet, no farm animals have been around.

The bloody horseshoe grave.

Stages Pond State Nature Preserve
5070 Hagerty Road
Ashville, Ohio 43103
39.670930, -82.933376

Dead Mules Rising

A wagon and team of mules lay at the bottom of Stage's Pond outside Ashville. A story about their haunting the pond area has been passed down from a local family to volunteers and staff at the preserve and verified by a descendant of the farmer.

Stages Pond is an extensive state nature preserve in mid-Ohio. It has both a wheel-chair accessible boardwalk and dirt trails. And it has ghosts. Because sometimes, when a storm rolls over Stages Pond State Nature Preserve, you can hear the resounding thud of horse hooves bolting across muddy roads and then the splash of swampy water as if something huge is bursting headlong into the boggy marsh there. Then, panicked horse screams echo in the air before they vanish as if swallowed up.

I know because I heard the shrieks of those horses one day while hiking the trail as thunderclouds crept across the sky and lightning came right after. As a horse owner and lover, I cannot shake it from my mind. When a stormy night comes on, and I'm taking in a lonesome trail, their cries still come to my ears. It is as if they follow me in my thoughts, and I cannot let them go.

I am not alone. More than one visitor to the preserve has been startled by this eerie turmoil. When they ask locals, they don't always believe the truth—that on a muggy August day in the 1800s, a farmer who lived across Ward Road was taking in the hay. A storm blew across the fields, and he ran to get out of the rain. Lightning bolted across the sky, along with a grand explosion of thunder right after. The wagon team he used to take in the hay bolted down over the road and across the muddy land around Stage's Pond. They went straight into the marshy, quick-sand-like muck, mired and fighting until they sank so deeply they could not be rescued. And now, only their ghostly echoes fill the thick air on hot summer nights, and right before a storm when lightning fills the sky and thunder rolls nearby. I know. I heard it.

Still-house Hollow
Keller-Kirn Park
Stringtown Road Northeast
Lancaster, Ohio 43130
39.738326, -82.600946

A Place Called Still-house Hollow

Still-house Hollow—

Long ago, a rugged path wove past family farms in Lancaster near the rear of the Poor House and ended where Rising Park is now. Its path roughly follows Stringtown Road, but it was named Foglesong Road back in the day for the family whose farm abutted a large portion of the road. A deep and dark valley along a place dubbed Flat Rocks was called Still-House Hollow, for it was known to have a whiskey still-house within. Most avoided this section after dark, for peculiar wails and screams came from this hollow. Some complained that they often could not shake a certain sensation of gloom when coming out the other side.

One night in the 1800s, Jacob Spangler, who lived on Foglesong Road, was taking an anxious horse ride along that rutted road to summon a doctor for a sick family member. He descended the forested hill leading into the hollow when his horse made a frightened snort, fixed her front legs hard in the soil, and quivered violently. Spangler leaned forward and squinted into the darkness. But what did his eyes behold? It was a yearling steer in his path with strangely glowing eyes and long hair. He tried to urge his horse forward, but the usually fearless mare refused to budge. Spangler started to turn her around. But before the two could change direction, he felt something seize his leg and upon looking down, he could see this *thing*—this half-man, half-calf was climbing up! Spangler could not move while the beast sat behind him, placing his front hooves over his shoulders. There the two rode until the boundary of the hollow, where the strange calf jumped off and disappeared into the woods. The dark hollow where Jacob Spangler came face to face with the half-man half-calf was where a traveler discovered a bloody trail in years past. A horse had come home without its rider, a man named Ornsdorff. Nothing was left except two empty saddlebags with a dried gummy mix of blood, brains, and hair stuck to them.

Would you dare to walk the Still-house Hollow trail?

A search party had followed the blood to the top of the hill and could see from the marks in the grass and soil where the man had fallen from his horse. They continued, following the path where it appeared a body was sloppily dragged from the road and into the dark hollow until they came to a shack with a still nearby owned by an old man named Crowley. The doors were locked, but the men broke through and resumed their pursuit of the bloody trail into a rear room. A foul stench of death and moldering sent some running out the door. When the rest entered the threshold of the room, before them lay a bloody corpse, but it was not a man and, instead, that of a dead yearling steer. The bodies of the homeowner and the dead rider were never found.

Even today, on certain nights, those driving along Stringtown Road feel a certain gloom embrace them until they reach Lancaster proper. Others hiking the trail note with a curious fascination that birds stop chirping and the air becomes oppressive in a particular area of the old hollow before the surroundings darken ominously around them. The aura becomes, well, unnerving. Why do they sense it? They do not know. But I know, and now you know, too.

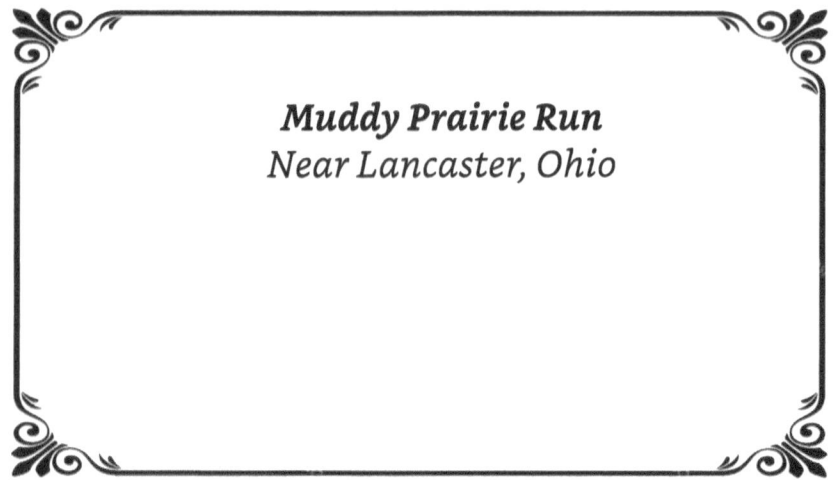

Muddy Prairie Run
Near Lancaster, Ohio

Ghostly Old Man on a Mule with a Keg of Rum

Muddy Prairie Run—right

In the early days, an old distillery was along a stream known as Muddy Prairie Run in Hocking Township of Fairfield County. The stream was small and used as a guide for those who traveled when there weren't so many roads. A well-worn trail beside it kept those on horseback on the path. There was good reason to keep to the old trace as around it, the land was known for the small pockets of boggy areas that were much avoided as a rider and horse could easily step into a particular quagmire and get sucked forever deep into its muck.

During this era, an old man, a regular fixture in the community, would mount his faithful old mule and traverse the Muddy Prairie Run to the distillery in the evenings. He would collect his keg of rum, a task he had faithfully performed for years. While there, he would share tales of the past, telling stories far into the night. When the establishment was ready to close, he would, with his keg securely fastened to the mule's rear, mount his steed and, perhaps a bit tipsy, make his way home along the stream.

After many years of the old man's regular visits to the distillery and his nightly rides home, he mysteriously vanished. As time passed, a road and school were built along the route, and houses popped up nearby. During this time, the ghost of an old man astride a small mule with a keg fastened to its saddle was sighted along the road near the creek and old school. It would veer slightly in its path near the bog and disappear. It was suspected that one night, the old man had gotten too drunk and veered off his path into a boggy patch, was swallowed up, and never seen again. Well, that is, except for his ghost.

Old Logan Road SE
Sugar Grove, Ohio 43155
39.620239, -82.552987

Dead Peddler of Sugar Grove

Old Logan Road—

A peddler haunts the Old Logan Road in Sugar Grove between Lancaster and Logan. It was right around 1815 when the ghostly form began to appear, scaring away carriage riders and farmers traveling this main road. Back then, Sugar Grove was little more than a few cabins dotting the wooded hillsides and not the pretty village it is now.

Pierre Bordeau, of French descent, made himself comfortable in a shabby little place by the road. It was along the hillside not far from the location the Sharp family sells pumpkins in the cooler days of autumn and around Halloween these days.

It would be Pierre's shack that a peddler would stop and ask for a night's sleep along his route. But over the next few days after, those who usually bought from the peddler noted he had not visited their homes. Many believed he had probably left Pierre's cabin during the night, so he did not have to pay for his lodging. There were no signs that would call up an alarm of any foul crime save a small pool of blood found by a spring near the road.

Years would pass, and whispers always kept travelers away from Pierre's cabin. Nobody wanted to stay there for rest. It seemed the water in the spring tasted bad, and you know, they didn't want to end up dead. And there was a certain rumor of a ghost haunting the road and hillside, popping out at carriage riders taking the Logan Road route, which was the only rugged path that once ran a straight drive from Lancaster to Logan. The ghost disappeared at the old spring.

Of course, no one suspected Pierre of murder. He was considered kind-hearted and had caused no one else any harm. But on his deathbed, he confessed to killing the peddler but refused to divulge the place where he had buried the poor man. Authorities searched the area for bones but found nothing save a decayed backpack with jewels and the old peddler's clothing. There was no sign of him until nearly seventy years later when, in the 1870s, owners of the property dug a new well along the hillside. Upon excavation, workers discovered a rotted corpse beneath some fieldstones.

The family whose farm was on the land quickly gave the remains a proper burial, and the hopes were that the ghost would find peace. But many years later, farmers coming through the area after dark still took a two-mile detour of that lonely spot on the Logan Road to avoid the ghost of the peddler.

Allen's Knob
Shallenberger Nature Preserve
Becks Knob Road SW
Lancaster, Ohio 43130
Allen's Knob: 39.691742, -82.657292
Bridge over Hunter's Run:
39.697397, -82.657292

Allen's Knob Lone Grave

The roadway and bridge over Hunter's Run, center, where a ghost walks. Allen's Knob far left.

Outside of Lancaster, on terrain that was once miles of rolling farmland are a series of tree-covered knobs of Blackhand sandstone that mark the edge of the Appalachian plateau—Beck's Knob, Allen's Knob, Claypool Knob, and Ruble Knob.

According to legend, once an old hermit spent much of his days reading the bible and looking out over the farmland from atop the rocky hill of Allen's Knob. He lived somewhere below in the shadows between the two knobs of Beck's and Allen's. As the sun would set, he would make his way down the hill, whistling all the way, to the small hollow of woodland to sleep in a shack among the large rocks littering the forest floor. He bothered no one. And no one bothered him.

Sitting on the knob where the old hermit once read his bible and near the shallow grave legends say he is buried. You can hike to the top too. Allen's Knob is at Shallenberger Nature Preserve.

For many years, the old hermit lived there. At some point, he became unhappy and decided to end his life. He began digging a grave at the top of Allen's Knob for himself. Sometime during the winter, he took up his flintlock rifle and killed himself, shooting a lead ball right through his heart. But before the hermit died, he left a note stating that he wished his remains buried in the spot he had dug atop the knob.

The roadway and bridge over Hunter's Run.
While driving past, look for the ghost!

For years, passersby would often say they saw the ghost of the old hermit wandering down a trail from Allen's Knob and along Beck's Knob Road until it came to a bridge at Hunter's Run. An old Lancaster resident would tell the story of how he met the ghost one Sunday evening riding his horse on his way to visit his sweetheart. The young man came upon the hermit about halfway down the hill just above Hunter's Run and extended a hand, asking him if he wished to hop on the horse with him, and he could take him to his destination. As the hermit grabbed his hand, his fingers were ice cold. Too late, the young man realized the old hermit was long-dead. The two rode down the hill, the young man badly frightened and begging the ghost to dismount, but the hermit would not speak. Trying to dislodge the ghostly rider, he began to use his whip, but the leather strap went right through the hermit's body. It was not until they crossed Hunter's Run that the ghost vanished.

Schiller Park
Schiller Statue
1069 Jaeger Street
Columbus, Ohio 43206
39.942155, -82.993550

Headless Man of Schiller Park

Schiller Monument—

On November 30, 1894, two young men were returning from a party, and they took a shortcut through a dark, deserted park in the German Village section of Columbus. Just within the park's bounds, they noticed a short figure draped in a gray robe that fell from shoulders to knees. He was pacing back and forth with hands outstretched along the walkway directly in front of the Schiller Monument, a park statue built in honor of the early German-American immigrant and playwright. Curious, the two paused.

One man named Sedinger grabbed the other, William Bell, and wheezed, "See, he ain't got no head!" Sure enough, the two grasped the robed figure was headless!

Over the weeks following, others walking through the park saw this robed, headless ghost wandering with arms flailing. Years have passed, and those visiting Schiller Park have occasionally seen it too. The ghost's existence is explained as this: In mid-November of 1894, a 54-year-old wine agent for Brandt and Company in Toledo named Albert Dittelbach was visiting the city of Columbus for business. Those around him noticed he was somewhat downcast, but no one expected to find him dead in the famous Schiller Park in German Village. He had committed suicide by shooting himself in the head.

Northeast Ohio

> ### *Erie Street Cemetery*
> *2254 East 9th Street*
> *Cleveland, Ohio 44115*
> *41.497039,-81.683654*

Joc-O-Sot

The grave of Joc-O-Sot

Among the lingering spirits in Erie Street Cemetery is Joc-O-Sot, chief of the Sauk. Despite his involvement in the Black Hawk War, he later transitioned into a fishing guide along the lakeshore. Joc-O-Sot died in 1844 at the age of 34. He wanted his remains to be taken to the northern U.S. He was not. Bound to Cleveland for eternity, he is among the ghostly figures sighted by cemetery visitors. Legend has it that Joc-O-Sot's rage over his burial site caused the earth to shake, shattering his gravestone. While a new marker has been put in place, the broken stone still remains visible.

Cuyahoga County
Jackass Hill
End of Praha Avenue
Cleveland, Ohio 44127
41.478804, -81.656823
Euclid Beach Park
16301 Lakeshore Boulevard
Cleveland, Ohio 44110
41.583997, -81.568897

Cleveland's Mad Butcher of Kingsbury Run

Old "Jackass Hill" near the end of Praha Avenue and Kingsbury Run where a Cleveland shanty town was located during the Great Depression and became the hunting grounds for a killer.

Cleveland was a gruesome playground for a mysterious serial killer called the Mad Butcher of Kingsbury Run between 1934 and 1938. The murderer killed at least a dozen shanty-town dwellers, drifters, and prostitutes. Many of the bodies were discovered in Kingsbury Run, a slum section of the Cleveland area running along a creek ravine near railroad tracks. The slayer began the butchery on the shores of Lake Erie and into Jackass Hill and ended the romp at the Lakeshore Dump.

Unfortunately, authorities from around the U.S. never caught the criminal. Some believe the Mad Butcher's ghost still creeps through the city. Many think the spirits of the victims return to the places the killer dumped them. Whether you believe in the spooks or not, the horrible circumstances around the murders will send chills through even the most hardened souls.

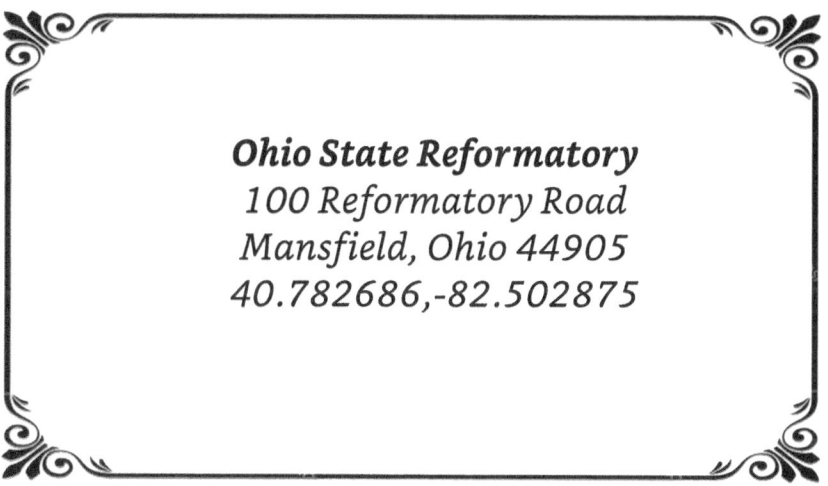

Ohio State Reformatory
100 Reformatory Road
Mansfield, Ohio 44905
40.782686,-82.502875

The Prison of the Dead

A ghostly guard walks through the image—

I have visited the Ohio State Reformatory a couple of times. Each time, something unique and ghostly transpires. Once, when my youngest son was 4, and we passed a certain cell, I was chatting with whoever was standing beside me.

My son quickly nudged me with forefinger to lips because, as he put it: "Mommy, there's a man trying to sleep in that bed." Oh. I looked. The bed was quite empty to my eyes. Another time, I took a picture of my daughter with a full-body apparition showing up in the image behind her. It was most certainly a spirited guard from long ago, we decided, rushing along the hallway. I have been touched there, and an old ghostly man whispered, "Please leave me alone," in my ear, and I caught it on a recording.

Is the old prison haunted? I think so. With so many bad people entering its walls and stuck there while alive, there has to be some sort of energy lingering. When the Ohio State Reformatory in Mansfield was open from 1896 to 1990, over 154,000 inmates passed through the gates. In addition, the prison took in offenders who were too old for juvenile corrections or who also committed less severe crimes than those sent to prison at the Ohio State Penitentiary in Columbus. The goal of this institution was to reform inmates with education, religion, and learning trades.

The reformatory was not always successful, and not everyone made it out alive. Two hundred people died at the jail, including guards killed in escape attempts. Frank Hanger, a 48-year-old guard, was beaten to death with an iron bar by Chester Probaski and Elza Chandler in October of 1932. He was making rounds in the disciplinary block, and Chandler crouched near a cupboard. Chandler was on an extended stay in solitary confinement. Prison wardens shuffled both murderers to the electric chair.

Even outside its walls, there was a tragedy. In July of 1948, Robert Daniels and 22-year-old John West, former prisoners, kidnapped and murdered John Niebel, his wife Nolana, and their 21-year-old daughter, Phyllis. John Niebel had been superintendent of the 1600-acre honor farm for 20 years. The men planned the revenge murder for four years.

Lyons Falls
Mohican State Park
Park Road
Perrysville, Ohio 44864
Trailhead:
40.613150, -82.316760

The Legend of Lyons Falls

Lyons Falls—
Mohican

Many years ago, a man named Paul Lyons lived a quiet life in a remote cabin in the rugged area now known as Mohican State Forest with his wife and son. He hunted and fished and earned some extra money by working at local farms or logging.

Some legends say that one night, his cow did not return to the barn during a storm. He called for her, his lantern in hand, to light the meager path. But the raucous clatter of rain hitting the autumn tree canopy above him and the wind blowing up through the valley below seemed to drown out the ting-ting of her cowbell. Still, at times, he could hear the faint ringing. He found himself along the cliff edge too late at some point along the trail. He lost his footing and fell to his death. On moonless nights, you can still hear him calling that cow and see his lantern waving above the cliff.

As with folklore, with the telling, sometimes a story gets skewed along the way. That said, the written historical account paints a different picture of his death, and one no less tragical for our ghostly tale. Around 1856, Paul Lyons was hauling logs one day and met a gruesome accident that resulted in his death and a grisly aftermath. Mister Lyons was buried, at first, on the hill between the two waterfalls. A marker once showed his grave. Then, later, a physician exhumed, stole, and mounted the skeleton of the poor man for display in his office. All that remains today is a depression in the earth. Oh, the light still shines along the hillside, and sometimes the man's ghost still shows, most likely poor Mister Lyons, looking for his corpse!

When walking along the trail near the waterfall, I was taking videos. I quickly stopped as not to be intrusive when I saw a person awkwardly sitting central to the picture who rose up, stepped to the path, and vanished!

Elliot Family Farmstead & Cemetery -West Branch State Park
Cable Line Road (CR-120)
Bloody Corners, Ohio 44266
Parking: 41.130559, -81.121185
Cemetery: 41.129817, -81.127267

Witch's Grave

The cemetery—before the vandals. From the Akron Beacon Journal

The cemetery—now

The lonely ruins of the Elliott Family Cemetery at West Branch State Park are barely visible, buried deep within the forest and along an almost-gone road. In the 1920s, when The Elliot Lake Club discovered this graveyard while clearing the land for a recreation area, it was dubbed "Portage's Lost Cemetery." The abandoned cemetery was attached to the old farmstead of long-departed Mulford and Betsy Elliott when it was common for folks to bury their dead not far from their backyards in family plots.

Remnants of that home are hardly a stone's throw away across a creek running between the two. As years passed, the U.S. Army Corps gobbled up this little piece of land for flood control, and the State of Ohio built West Branch State Park in 1965. While the park was developing, it was not just hikers discovering the lonely graveyard and the skeleton of the old home. Others with less respectful intentions found the solitary cemetery and the peculiar grave of a 17-year-old. Her headstone had a haunting message of death and dying: *Remember youth as you pass by, As you are now, so once was I.* The morbid words are an old Latin saying used by Greeks and Romans in their epitaphs—Quod tu es, ego fui, quod ego sum— "What you are I once was, what I am, you will become."

Just across the creek, too, there was a mysterious pile of stones. Now, everyone knew settlers were intolerant of witches, getting rid of them by burying their remains outside consecrated grounds with a slab of rock placed on top to keep them from climbing out of the grave as revenants, walking corpses that might harm those still living. The curious heard the stories, and they sought the boneyard out, searching for this witch's grave. In May of 1969, vandals desecrated the old graveyard. They broke headstones and left beer cans strewn across the old hallowed grounds.

After, those who vandalized the cemetery came to all sorts of bad luck. Anyone who took something from the land met with bad fortune. As the story goes, a witch's grave lies in the forest. Neighbors accused a young woman of being a witch. Those in town forced her into the woods. They laid her down, placed boards on top, then buried her beneath massive slabs of stones to kill her—so she could not rise again. But she did. Now, you can see the ghostly form of the witch roaming the dark forest. And if you peer into the depths of one stone slab, dead-red eyes stare back at you.

I parked just off the buckled asphalt of Cable Line Road where the road is blocked by a gate. At the gate, I followed the old street Line Road near the gate to the second marked trail to the right, D Loop Trail, which quickly intersects Machine Trail. At the junction of these two trails, I went straight (D Loop) about 30 steps, and found the location of the Elliott House to the left. This is one area with the stacked rocks that some believe is the Witch Grave.

After returning to the latter intersection and turning left, I followed Machine Loop Trail around the old property and the cemetery. Then I turned left on Yellow Trail. Once back on the road (looped), I turned left and walked to the top of the small hill on the roadway, and there was a trail (41.129167, -81.126700) to the left leading to the old cemetery (41.129817, -81.127267).

Just around the corner is an old orchard of the Elliot family that became a quarry. It is now the Quarry Trail at West Branch SP. Several different witnesses have adamantly told me the old quarry is haunted by a worker killed there. I could find little background on the quarry, but sometimes that is the case. However, I hiked the rugged path a couple of times and it worth checking out! (41.127464, -81.121305)

Beaver Creek State Park
Jake's Lock
Off Sprucevale Road
East Liverpool, Ohio 43920
40.706094, -80.582595

Jake's Lock: Dead Night Watchman

Jake's Lock—

Night watchmen would man the locks for boat traffic during the canal years after dark. One man named Jake was performing his nightly duties when a thunderstorm swept through. He grabbed his lantern and hurried along the lock to retreat to cover, but he was struck by lightning and died instantly. Dead but not entirely gone, Jake still walks this lock with his lantern, a tiny light bobbing after dusk.

Beaver Creek State Park
Parking:
Farthest Lot
Off Sprucevale Road
East Liverpool, Ohio 43920
40.705086, -80.585143

Gretchen's Lock

Gretchen's Lock

E.H. Gill was the chief canal engineer and a Royal Engineer's School graduate in Paris who traveled by ship from France with his wife and 7-year-old daughter, Gretchen, to help build the Sandy and Beaver Canal. Tragedy struck halfway to the United States when Gill's wife was washed overboard and drowned. Grief-stricken, the father and daughter continued to their new life. Gill worked with the Sandy and Beaver Canal system and helped build the lock above Sprucevale. His daughter followed him from camp to camp, living in the wild area around the new canal.

During this time, Gretchen contracted malaria. One afternoon, as her fever mounted, she made her father promise to take her home and bury her with her mother—"I want to join my mother," she pleaded. Wanting to please her, the father nodded that, indeed, he would. But, before the day ended, Gretchen was dead.

Temporarily, workers prepared a crypt in the masonry of Lock 41 just above Sprucevale, and Gretchen was interred in a small casket there. A major recession in the U.S. economy occurred in 1837, and Gill resigned from his position to return to Europe. He took Gretchen's body from her interim tomb in the lock and placed it on the ship to return home for reburial. However, the vessel Gill was sailing on was lost at sea during a storm on the return voyage. He and Gretchen would join her mother just as she begged him to do. Still, Gretchen returns to the lock once in a while, murmuring her dying prayer, "Bury me with my mother."

Beaver Creek State Park
Hambleton's Mill
Sprucevale Road
Negley, Ohio 44441
40.706900, -80.580732

The Ghost of Esther Hale

The old mill—

In the early 1800s, the Hambleton brothers purchased a grist mill and platted out the town of Sprucevale, which thrived until the mid-1800s and the fading of the canal boom. The grist mill remains today, home to a ghostly woman named Esther Hale. Hale came from Carmel Church of the Orthodox Friends.

She was among the first of these robust Pennsylvania preachers. She was a hard worker who toiled among the Sandy and Beaver Canal laborers, advising temperance among the rowdy canal men. Whenever Hale would preach, she would call out for those in her audience: "Follow me down the path to salvation!" On St. Nicholas's Eve, December 5th of each year, the ghost of Preacher Hale appears at the old Hambleton grist mill dressed in white. She scratches "Come" on the wall of the old stone grist mill before she leads those watching inside and vanishes.

Well, of course I had to peer inside to see if Esther was there!

Blue Bridge
Township Hwy 118
(Lamereaux Road)
Norwalk, Ohio 44857
41.279413, -82.675063

The Grim Apparition at Blue Bridge of Samuel Seymour

The Blue Bridge—

During the War of 1812, a blockhouse was built in Milan to protect area settlers from attacks by Native Indian raiders. When the fort was there, two young men—18-year-old Samuel Seymour and 15-year-old Reuben Pixley, Jr. set out from the blockade to cut down a bee tree to get the wax and the sweet treat of the honey within. They made their way to the tree's location on the south side of a small stream that met with the West Branch of the Huron River and began taking the tree down.

When they were just about finished with their job, they were fired upon by Indians. Seymour was instantly killed. Pixley got entangled in some brush as he tried to escape and was taken prisoner, where he remained in captivity for several months.

Later, the small creek where Seymour was killed would be named Seymour Creek. And this area, where it meets with the West Branch of the Huron, is haunted by Samuel Seymour. Early on, people taking Lamereaux Road and crossing the bridge, now called the Blue Bridge, over the West Branch of the Huron River would see little lights working their way through the valley where the young settler was murdered. Mist forms in the little pocket of the valley even during dry seasons, hazy lights dance along the banks and hillside where Samuel Seymour died, and some passing along the bridge have even seen a man's dark and grim silhouette there.

Salem Reformed Cemetery
Township Road 110
Millersburg, Ohio 44654
40.513669, -81.841397

Angel of Death

Angel of Death

Just a mile from the small community of Saltillo, the Salem Reformed Church once stood along with its cemetery. Of the many graves at the church cemetery, one stands out among the others. It is a 15-foot tall monument topped with a 5-foot angel draped in drooping branches of evergreen. The angel was placed over the grave of Mary Conrad by her husband, George—a prosperous farmer with land south of the cemetery when she died at 57 years of age in April of 1890. Later, his family buried George beside her beneath the monument.

After World War I, the congregation had grown older or scattered in many directions, and the church was eventually demolished. Only the lonely cemetery remains on the hilltop with the legendary angel, now headless. In earlier years, folklore began to spread that this angel was an instrument of death; those who met her gaze at midnight would soon die. As a rite of passage, high school teens would gather as a group, daring each other to stand before the angel and waiting for her head to turn—whoever her eyes laid upon would die.

The angel now stands forlorn and vandalized over the years—her wings and hands broken. Her head is gone, stolen many times, but always returned as she tends to eke out little bits of revenge on those who hurt her. Once, police were investigating a fatal car crash. When they opened the trunk of the vehicle, they found the angel's head—the teen who had stolen it ended up dead. Enough was enough—trustees secreted her head in a safer place. She is known to take flight; even with her wings mangled, she flits around the cemetery in the dark.

Ruins of Swift Mansion -
Light and Hope Orphanage
52374 Gore Orphanage
Road
Amherst, Ohio 44001
41.355052, -82.335234

Gore Orphanage

Remains of Gore Orphanage—

Johnathon Swift built a mansion on land along Gore Road (named for the triangular shape). It was later the home of the Wilber family, and after it caught the eye of John Sprunger, a wealthy industrialist/builder, and his wife, Katie, who founded the Light and Hope Missionary Society in 1893 and the Light and Hope Orphanage and added on nearby homes and properties. While many believed the enterprise was charitable, it was a lucrative business using orphans as free labor, workers in his printing shop and on his farm.

The orphans were also farmed out to the community to earn money for the business. Up to 125 children, watched by wardens/overseers at a time, were used for slave labor. They were underfed and overworked. The orphanage stayed open until 1916. The old mansion was burned down in 1923 by the homeless taking up residence. Since then, there have been stories of a ghost child swinging on an old tree and children's giggles or sobbing sweeping through the woods. While carrying a recorder at Gore Orphanage, I heard a child's voice say softly, "Tryphenia"—that is how I found out about the Swift's children, researching what the word meant and finding it was a name of their daughter, Tryphenia, who died at age five in 1831 and is buried nearby.

Louiza Catherine Fox
Murder Site
Twp Hwy 546 B (Starkey Road)
Barnesville, Ohio 43713
40.104476,-81.174702

IT Came

The place where something bad happened—

Something peculiar lurks in a wild pocket of overgrown scrub meadows mixed with deep, young woodland in Belmont County, Ohio. It is just off Interstate 70, and those who pass along the highway usually sense there is more to the land than meets the eye. It has an uninviting appearance in certain areas, and justly so. The once-rich land was stripped clean by seventy years of surface mining. It left it a bleak and barren wasteland, inhospitable and desolate. Its terrain was so deeply gashed and gouged that it was unidentifiable from the once tidy rolling hillsides of yesteryears.

Not so long in the past, when little more was left to steal from the earth, the Ohio Division of Wildlife bought up the dying property, revived the land, and allowed it to heal and grow back to its wild self again. But not all the earth appeared to grasp this fresh start. Those with a keen perception take note, in a particular section, that something had changed, shifted, and altered during its plundered past. It was as if peeling back the flesh of the terrain, then gouging out the soul of the land, freed something wicked from the earth's bowels. Something long buried. Something that should never return. Something so dreadfully evil, it still walks as if the land beneath its feet is still quite . . . dead.

Something happened in this little pocket, and it transpired like this: Egypt Valley Wildlife Area was once a land of fertile farmland and forest wilderness. From the late 1820s to the early 1900s, it was home to the small and sparsely inhabited town of Egypt, with a population of about 10. Egypt was mainly known as a place where folks stopped to chat about the weather or crops. At the same time, their grain was ground into flour and middling, for it had a gristmill along the shallow Stillwater Creek.

Before this land was laid bare by mining, a small community dotted the hillside with homes and farmsteads—

A few homes were in the town proper, and the rest of its residents were settled on small homesteads for miles around it. It had a post office, schoolhouse, and small cemetery. A little Methodist Church was within a short buggy ride for those devout. It was within a few miles of this very town that a horrible murder occurred in the deep throes of the winter of 1869.

In the 1800s, it was common for young unmarried girls to work as housemaids to help their families and keep them busy before marriage, performing light housework like cleaning fireplaces, dusting the furniture, washing clothing, and generally picking up after those who lived in the household. Employers often provided the girls with room and board and a stipend for their work. Thirteen-year-old Louiza Fox did just that for a local coal mine owner, Alex Hunter, and his family, who lived in Sewellsville, just a few miles away from her father's farm. On the late afternoon of January 21st of 1869, while she was returning home from her employers, 22-year-old Thomas Carr, one of the miners in Hunter's employ, abruptly stopped her on the road.

The man, known locally for his drunken bouts, braggarting twaddle, and angry temper, had been pursuing the little girl relentlessly since the previous autumn. He had, several times, accompanied her from work to home. John Fox, Louiza's father, questioned Carr with a wary eye. Still, the miner insisted he only walked with Louiza to watch over her because of her tender age. Louiza refused any idea of courting the older man again and again. However, it was brought to her father's attention by Louiza herself that Carr had asked her to marry him some weeks earlier. The child asked her father to please refuse the peculiar, threatening, and unpleasant man; she had no interest in him. Although Louiza and her father both thwarted continued advances and gift-bestowing by Carr, his stalking had come to a head on that fateful day as he followed her from room to room at the Hunter home, asking her to marry him. Noting Carr's strange behavior, Louiza's employer tried to persuade the young girl to stay at the house for her safety until they could take her home by horseback. She refused.

When her 6-year-old brother, Willy, came to escort her home, she left with the boy, setting out around four or five in the afternoon. Carr attempted to waylay Louiza on her path home, and she tried desperately to elude him along the isolated roadway by running at some points. Then, as Louiza and her little brother passed a small chestnut orchard, which was a stone's throw from home, Carr made his move and crept from beside a fence by the trees and into their path. Carr asked the girl to marry him once again. She refused, telling him she was far too young to be wed. He then pulled a razor from his pocket, tossed her by one shoulder to the ground, and slit her throat.

By the time her father had hastened to the spot, he had found young Louiza lying dead in a small ditch by the road where Carr had dragged her during the short struggle. Carr was hunted down and eventually apprehended and hanged. Years later, the Hanna Coal Division of the Consolidation Coal Company would drive the living from their homes during a strip mine boom. They laid bare the farmland, barns, churches, houses, and old mills. They chewed a path through where Louisa grew up, lived, thrived, then died.

Their "GEM" machine, the name stands for "giant earth mover," stripped the land and nearly obliterated the township of Kirkwood. It took and took from the soul of the earth and dug and dug until it hit something dark and deep that comes with the same greed and gluttony and a lack of empathy of those who unearthed its ugly spirit. Because something remains—It is that dark thing that got dug up. IT lingers around a stone tucked into the Egypt Valley Wildlife Area, marking where Carr murdered Louiza. IT lurks along the roadway, creeping on an old path a happy little girl once took. IT stops. IT waits. Then IT moves toward a small hillside, then a ditch, and lingers there as if savoring that moment on January 21st, 1869, that others think is beyond horror, but IT feels delightful and savoring and sweet. Then, it disappears. Unless, of course, it sees someone else that catches ITS eyes.

Coshocton
Coshocton, Ohio 43812

The Old Oak Tree

The railroad in early years.

In the early days, when the Panhandle Railroad was being laid in Coshocton, shanty houses popped up outside town for the workers on the tracks and their families. A beautiful young woman named Mary Mulhaney, an Irish immigrant lived in one of these shanties. She fell in love with one of the young men in the settlement, but after some time, he deserted her for another. Distraught, she hanged herself from a giant oak tree. Time would pass, and several hunters paused beneath the tree one afternoon.

One among them shifted his gun; it blasted into the air, and he fell dead. The man, it was found, was the lover who shunned poor Mary Mulhaney. In no time, between the dead hours of night, 12 a.m. to 3 a.m., the figures of Mary, her lover, and a black dog would pass the old oak.

Bridge Over Sugar Creek
1694 OH-39
Dover, Ohio 44622
40.512649, -81.488303

The Sack Did Rise As Did the Ghost

The bridge over Sugar Creek where Mary would rise—

Ellen Athey was a member of a small, close-knit community in the farming area of Tuscarawas County. She was peevish, prone to sudden angry outbursts, jealous streaks, and demanding. Her husband Henry would buckle under her many orders and do whatever pleased his wife. In 1880, it would be hiring a young family member to help Ellen clean the home and care for herself and their children. The eighteen-year-old hireling was named Mary Seneff, a pretty and hard-working girl who set to the tasks appointed to her obediently.

It was the summer of that year that Ellen murdered poor Mary with an ax in a jealous and unwarranted rage, declaring Mary had made eyes at Henry. When the stench was overwhelming after burying the corpse in the yard, Ellen tried to burn the body in a fire. The rotting remains that had not burned well were then stuffed into a feed sack with Mary's calico dress, weighted with a brick, and tossed into Sugar Creek.

But the sack did rise, as did Mary's ghost within two weeks. Curious miners coming home from work wiggled the peculiar package to shore with a stick and opened it to expose the wretched remains. Ellen was found guilty. Mary was buried. Not long after, a ghostly woman began emerging from the stagnant waters of Sugar Creek, wearing a loosely fitting white gown and shuffling along the shoreline to the road whenever people passed. In one hand, she held a garment, and with the fingers of the other hand, she wiggled them near her neck to expose a huge gash. Then, she quietly strolled backward along the bank before returning to her watery grave.

Northwest Ohio

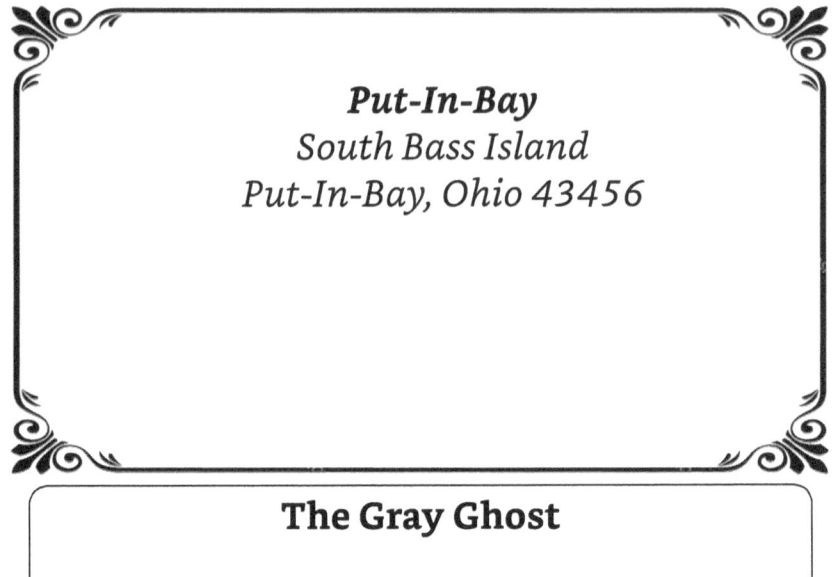

Put-In-Bay
South Bass Island
Put-In-Bay, Ohio 43456

The Gray Ghost

Looking out into the bay—

In the winter of 1926 to 1927, a ship ladened with illegal liquor left a Canadian port heading to the U.S. Then it vanished, believed to have gone down in a watery grave in Lake Erie during a winter storm. Two crew corpses had been discovered along a shoreline. Then, the ship returned ghostly and gray, whipping past Conneaut and Cleveland surrounded in fog. What's more, it was seen numerous times, persistently haunting the coastline of Put-In-Bay, adding to the mystery. It came to be known as "The Gray Ghost."

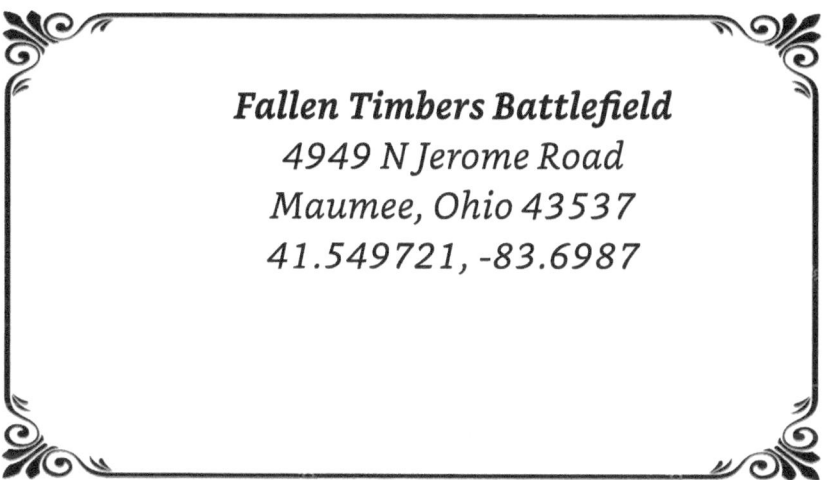

Fallen Timbers Battlefield
4949 N Jerome Road
Maumee, Ohio 43537
41.549721, -83.6987

Ghosts of Fallen Timbers Battlefield

A section of the loop trail at Fallen Timbers Battlefield—

When pioneers began to settle into Northwest Territory lands used by Native Peoples, such as Erie, Kickapoo, Odawa, and Wyandotte, the two began to clash violently. Members of the Delaware, Chippewa, Ottawa, Wyandot, and other tribes started an alliance to battle the settlers and American military. President George Washington would send General Anthony Wayne to lead troops into the Maumee River area near Toledo to fight the growing confederation of Ohio and Great Lakes Indian Tribes.

As the battle played out on August 20, 1794, and the American military pushed the warriors back, these Native Indians found shelter in timbers that had fallen during a tornado a few years earlier. Wayne's military eventually drove the Native Indian army out, resulting in a treaty forcing the tribes to give up land and move west.

Occasionally, around the anniversary of the war, ghostly soldiers play out the battle on stormy nights. But that is not all. Those who have visited the site have revealed their paranormal encounters to me over the years, from gentle but startling touches on the shoulder as they pass the area of the fallen timbers to seeing what they described as murky shadow figures appearing and disappearing in the woodland.

Buckland Lock (Lock 43)
Wabash and Erie Canal
Old US-24
Liberty Center, Ohio 43532
41.419817, -83.900076

Bill Bellington Won't Leave Buckland's Lock

Buckland's Lock

Ohio once had a series of locks along the Miami, Wabash, and Erie Canal system by the Maumee River near Grand Rapids at a canal boomtown called Providence. One section where boats could come in along the slack waters of Providence Dam of the river was a guard lock (a lock used to protect the canal from flood waters) called Buckland's Lock or just plain Lock 43. Here, boats from the Gilead Canal across the Maumee River could lock into the Miami & Erie Canal. Then, they could work through a series of locks, including Lock 43.

In the 1800s, when the canal was in use, as canal boatmen neared the Buckland Lock, they would hear cries and groans along the shoreline as if someone was in great pain. Louder it would get until a mist would rise from the canal waters before their boat. Then, the fog would form into the distinct, gaunt figure of a little old man. He would fumble around the sluice gates before stepping back and opening them wide. The boats would begin to pass through the lock only to find the gate closed. This strange occurrence would happen at each of the series of locks running this section of the canal, the old misty ghost reappearing and disappearing at each gate.

Locals used to explain the strange phenomenon like this:

The previous lock keeper at Providence during the 1880s was a heavy-drinking man named Bill Bellington. Near midnight, after drinking all day, there was a cry of alarm that Bellington's quarters were on fire. The next morning, locals discovered his charred body within his shack. Many believed that someone murdered him for money he had secreted within his home. For years after his death, the spirit of the little old man continued to work the locks; his ghost appeared to boatmen and others along the canal at Buckland's Lock.

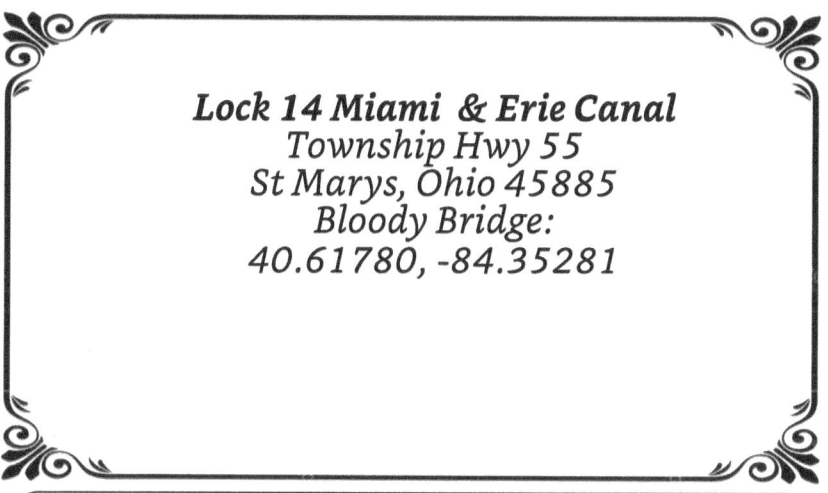

Lock 14 Miami & Erie Canal
Township Hwy 55
St Marys, Ohio 45885
Bloody Bridge:
40.61780, -84.35281

Bloody Bridge

At the Bloody Bridge—

In the mid-1800s, passenger packets and cargo boats traveled the waterway connecting the Ohio River and Lake Erie, called the Miami & Erie Canal, from Toledo to Cincinnati. A driver guided a mule that walked the towpath along the shore and pulled the boat. During the canal years, between Spencerville and St. Marys, two boats were commonly seen along the waterway—the Daisy and the Minnie Warren. Jack Billings was a big, softhearted man and a driver for the Daisy. A moody man named William Jones led the mules for the Minnie Warren.

The captain's daughter was on board this boat, and it was her name given to the packet. Minnie cooked for those on board and rode faithfully by her father's side on the canal route. Minnie and Jack often flirted playfully with each other as their boats passed. After some time, they both realized they loved each other. Jack counted the hours between the time Minnie's boat disappeared after passing and when he would see it appear in the distance again. Minnie felt her heart pound wildly when she shyly caught the man's eyes in hers while they teased each other about whose boat was the better. All of this flirting made William Jones jealous as he loved Minnie, too. William would have mentioned his liking to the young woman, but the driver knew she only had eyes for Jack Billings, and it would not have made a difference. So he just seethed over their fledgling relationship from sunup to sundown. He tossed and turned at night, dreaming up ways to get the girl all to himself.

It was not until one evening in the fall of 1854 that William's jealousy peaked after a social event both Minnie and Jack attended. Late in the evening, they paused at the bridge as they walked home along the canal. Little did they know William was waiting for them in the shadows with a sharp-edged ax. In one stroke, the bitter man cut Jack down. Minnie fell backward over the edge of the bridge and into the water below. She drowned in the murky waters of the canal. Some would say it was shock that sent her reeling to her death, but others believed the moment Jack died, she did not want to live at all and took the plunge to be with him. Soon after, someone stumbled upon the gruesome scene of Jack's lifeless body and noticed the girl floating dead in the water. They brought her body up and laid it next to the bloody corpse of her sweetheart. Gone, they were.

But each of the young lovers left their mark on the region. For nearly forty years after Jack's body was removed from the bridge, the bloodstains left from his body remained engraved in the wood. And hence, it received its name—Bloody Bridge. It has been passed down that those who looked into the water near the bridge where Minnie died said they would see her face staring up at them from beneath the muddy canal water.

I tried it from the bridge, then beneath it. This is me staring at the water after riding my bike along the trail to get to the location. That day, I only saw my own reflection.

Dr. Martin Luther King Jr.
Bridge
The Old Cherry Street
Bridge
1 Main Street
Toledo, Ohio 43605
41.651094,-83.526147

Plodding Ghost of Dr. Martin Luther King Jr. Bridge

Martin Luther King Bridge—

Occasionally, those crossing the Dr. Martin Luther King Jr. Bridge, the Old Cherry Street Bridge, spanning the Maumee River in Toledo have seen a barefoot man plodding silently across its length before he vanishes. He is dragging a rope along behind him. This apparition has been seen since the summer of 1882, even though the bridge has been rebuilt a few times since.

Few know that this ghost was once a local shoemaker, Joseph "Pop" Meyers, well-dressed except that he had no shoes on, who hanged himself there in 1882 with a piece of rope. His son asked the police if he could have the rope to remember his father. Soon after, the son used the same rope to hang himself in the same spot.

Goll Woods State Nature Preserve
County Road 26
Stryker, Ohio 43557
41.554640, -84.361394

The Feu Follet of Goll Woods

Goll Woods—

Tiny dancing balls of light appear in the dark and mosquito-ridden forest of Goll Woods near Archbold. The bugs and the magical should not be surprising in this little bit of old-growth woodland typical of the Great Black Swamp once covering this part of northwestern Ohio. Some speculate the lights could be bioluminescence, light emitted by insects like fireflies or plants like fungi through chemical reactions. Others believe they might come from something more ominous—something that lures the unsuspecting to the area, off the beaten path, and into the deepest and murkiest parts of the swampland, never to be found.

The existence of the latter is explained as this— In 1836, Peter and Catherine Goll and their 2-year-old son traveled from France to America, settling in this Black Swamp region of Ohio. For over 130 years, the family flourished, lived, loved, and died on their fertile farmland until a descendant sold the property to the state as a nature preserve. Throughout those years, tiny lights appeared in the marshy forest near the old family cemetery, homestead, and surrounding forest. It is not surprising. The family brought their traditions and lore along with them to their new country as in some regions of France during the Lenten season, the feu-follet (lights of the souls of unbaptized children) dance along the trails and roadways begging passersby to anoint them with a sprinkle of water. Occasionally, the mischievous sprites bewitch travelers, luring them into the swamp. Even animals may fall under the spell. Old-timers passed along that an early traveler riding by horseback had his mare enchanted by the light. The horse followed the tiny flicker, never to return, but a search party found the man half-dead the following day, wandering dazed in the bogs.

Those who knew this enduring tradition commented that a peculiarly large number of people disappeared without a trace in this part of Northwestern Ohio and noted that these little lights twinkling in the woods could be the cause! I took the trail, which was beautiful, but I did not get to pause to search for the mysterious Feu Follet, nor would it have been able to lure me into its domain. It was a hot summer day and humid after a quick summer thunderstorm. I forgot my bug spray and was probably more suitably dressed for the beach in my shorts and tank top than a walk through the swamp. I was but a quarter mile in when I realized my blunder. I sprinted the remaining way back without taking a breath, with arms waving wildly and mouth closed to not drink a thousand mosquitoes waiting for their next meal!

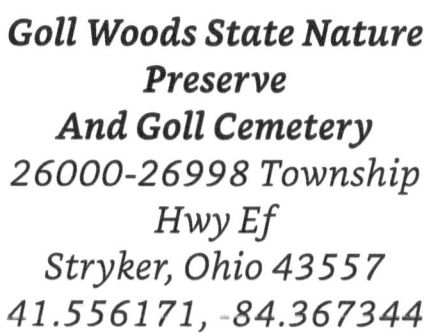

***Goll Woods State Nature
Preserve
And Goll Cemetery***
*26000-26998 Township
Hwy Ef
Stryker, Ohio 43557
41.556171, -84.367344*

Shhh! Don't Awaken Marieanne

Marieanne's grave—

The Goll Cemetery is within Goll Woods and by the nature preserve trail. If you take the trail and when passing by along your way, pause for just a moment for a breath. While you do, stand in front of Marieanne Goll's grave and say, "Hello." Perhaps you will awaken her spirit from its deathly slumber. It is said if you do, a mist will rise, forming into Marieanne before she travels slowly to nearby children's graves and weeps for their early deaths.

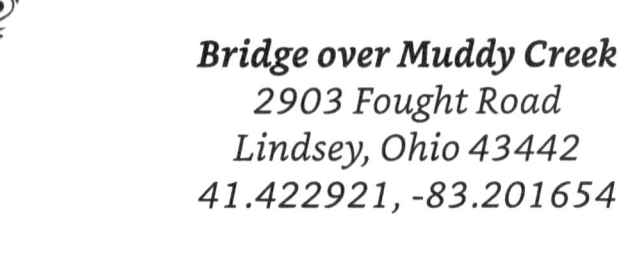

Bridge over Muddy Creek
2903 Fought Road
Lindsey, Ohio 43442
41.422921, -83.201654

Elmore Rider

A ghostly rider along the road where a legend emerged—

There is a ghost light about 30 miles from Toledo near the towns of Lindsey and Oak Harbor. Old legends relate a house was haunted by an old man who shot himself. He threatened beforehand to return after death.

A more recent version explains the lights with more romantic flair—it is about a couple who pledged their love to each other just as World War I broke out. The young man was sent off to war and fought overseas.

The two wrote back and forth for a year, long letters of love and heartache, and missing each other, then the letters from the man simply stopped coming. Heartbroken, the young woman was sure her sweetheart was dead. On March 21st of 1918, he returned from the war. Why he had not written his sweetheart, is not told. But to surprise the young woman as he neared her home, he shut off his motorcycle along the roadway the evening of his return and snuck to her window and peered inside. The woman who pledged her life to him was with another man. Distraught, the young man sped off on his motorcycle, not heeding his speed, nor ruts in the old farm road. Suddenly, the bike hitched, and he tumbled off near a small bridge over Muddy Creek. He was decapitated by barbed fence wire running along the fields. Now, legends tell that on March 21st each year, the Elmore Rider returns. People see ghostly lights along Fought Road, where it crosses Muddy Creek.

Republic Train Tracks
Tracks near S Kilbourne Street
Republic, Ohio 44867
41.119210, -83.021740

The Warning Light

The Republic train tracks—

On a cold January 4th, 1887, at 1:15 a.m., Lynn Fletcher, the conductor, was heading east from Tiffin in a freight train. The train was hauling 19 cars filled with barrel hoops and staves. The track was a single one, which meant that only one train could pass at a time. Fletcher was aware that the B & O Express Engine #726, a passenger train from New York to Chicago, was also on the same track heading west. He knew that he needed to make an easy stop at the passing siding in Republic to allow the faster express train to safely pass.

However, the temperatures were falling fast and dropped to nearly ten degrees below zero. Fletcher's older, cumbersome freight train came upon an incline in the track and, due to the cold, began to lose steam. Realizing it was moving too slowly and the other train, moving at 60-miles-per-hour, was going to be coming before he could make the spur, Conductor Fletcher climbed up on the freight cars to flag the train to stop. It was sooner than expected that the conductor saw the passenger train rounding a bend. Desperately, he lifted his lantern in warning to the passenger train engineer, Lem Eastman. Eastman hit the brakes, but the two trains collided. Only the anguished cries of the passengers within the oncoming train filled the air along with the explosion of metal to metal.

The number of passengers killed may never be known, but estimates remain at 15 to 19 dead. People in the nearby village buried the unclaimed and unidentified (many burned beyond recognition) in the nearby Farewell Retreat Cemetery in Republic. But the story of the ill-fated train would not end there.

In just a few months, small lights started appearing along the tracks. One evening, as the Express No 5 train neared the site of the wreck, the engineer spotted a red light—a distress signal waving in the air. He applied the brakes and reversed the engines, bringing the train to a stop right at the exact spot of the train wreck. However, when they arrived, there was no one there, and the light had disappeared. Prior to the train stopping, both the engineer and the fireman claimed they saw the person carrying the lantern—a woman wearing a filmy white dress. Other engineers have also reported seeing this apparition, and ghostly lights continue to appear where the train wreck took place, all the way to the cemetery and the location of the unknown graves.

Harrod Cemetery and Highway 56
4900 Township Highway 56
Bellefontaine, Ohio 43311
40.423173, -83.782884

Hatchet Man

Highway 56, where a ghostly hatchet man searches for prey.

Andrew Hellman was a tailor who arrived in America from Germany in 1817. To most with whom he crossed paths, he was well-mannered, good-looking, and had many friends. He married Mary Abel— blithe, buxom, and light-hearted. Within a short time, he had built up a business and a farm on Township Highway 56 outside Huntsville. The couple had three children—two boys and a girl. One April morning of 1839, after his children had grown, Louisa (age 17), Henry (age 16), and John (age 12) awakened quite ill. Within a day, Louisa and John both died and were buried together in a grave.

At some point after her children's deaths, Mary recalled picking up a jug of milk, and upon seeing a powdery substance on it, she decided not to drink the liquid. It occurred to her that someone may have poisoned her children. She kept the idea to herself, only once mentioning her fears to a sister in a note. It was, perhaps, too horrendous a thought the children's father would murder them. Or maybe it was fear. Unbeknownst to all around them, Mary and the children had been suffering horribly at Andrew's hand.

The following month, Mary sent her only surviving son, Henry, to live with her brother, George. Several days passed, and no one heard from Mary. Finally, George's wife went to check on her. She found Andrew Hellman alive and lying on the bed covered in blood and Mary's mutilated body lying on the floor, an ax slicing through her skull.

Andrew was questioned and jailed, but he fled to Maryland, changed his name to Adam Horn, and started anew with a farm. Then, he married a young girl, Malinda, who was only 16 years old. On a stormy, snowy night in March 1843, Andrew Hellman murdered his second wife in cold blood. He dismembered her body and hid the parts throughout the farm in old coffee bags and a trunk. This time, when arrested for the murder, Andrew was convicted and executed for his crimes. He was buried in an unmarked grave at Harrod Cemetery.

Those who heard his story also gave him the name of Hatchet Man. Nearly a thousand spectators came to watch him hang. But just as many have probably driven along Township Highway 56 past Harrod Cemetery looking for his ghost. Some nights, his spirit runs along the street, a hatchet in his hand, waiting for some unknowing Samaritan to stop and give him a ride.

For Those Who Like to Seek Out Ghosts

Seeking Ghosts: Why do ghost hunters use certain tools?

Energy is the capacity to do work
and is all around us—

*Kinetic energy is energy that an object has when in motion.

*Potential Energy is stored energy (not moving, but can release energy when acted upon)

Some forms of energy are:

Thermal (heat)

Electromagnetic (energy from light or electromagnetic waves)

Gravitational Energy (potential energy dependent upon gravitational field)

Ghost hunters believe that spirits can manipulate this energy. We know from Newton's Law that *objects at rest stay at rest. Objects in motion stay in motion. . . Unless acted on by some external force.* When objects move, or a piece of equipment developed to detect these energies sets off an alarm, we try to explain these reasons and find that force. Suppose we cannot explain why the object moved or if the alarm detected a specific energy. In that case, we communicate to see if it is, perhaps, a ghost manipulating the power and being that force. One theory is that the conscious mind has an electromagnetic field that does not expire when we die. This field has a current that can be detected.

Be Patient. Respect the Dead.

Throughout my 30-year experience, I've learned that everyone has their own beliefs about paranormal exploration. The more places you visit and the more frequently you visit them, the higher the likelihood of having supernatural experiences. However, it's important to note that despite visiting a place multiple times, having no experience is still possible. In contrast, someone visiting for the first time could have a significant experience. In the realm of the paranormal, ghosts operate on their own terms and are not influenced by the length of time one has been attempting to make contact with them. Or who it is. Ultimately, it's up to them to decide when and how they will reveal themselves. That said, I do believe that ghosts tend to migrate toward people with whom they can identify in some way, whether it is something that they "see" in you or "feel," I do not know! They were once just like you and me, good and bad and angry or happy. That said, respect the dead. Don't be a jerk and disrespect or try to angrily provoke them. It is just ridiculous to think making something mad will draw a *spirit* out.

Do Your Research. Dig Deeper.

One of the main points about ghost hunting or just enjoying the folklore and ghost stories—do your background research. I cannot tell you how many places I have visited and watched people exploring the ghostly side—in the *wrong* place or trying to cull out the *wrong* ghost. Recently, while I was providing a ghost tour at the famous Moonville Tunnel, a band of paranormal enthusiasts with a "psychic" came in and set up boundless equipment (including a laser light grid expanding out into the woods and sky with adults/children running around with no eye protection), spending the evening ghost hunting—*in an area that was not even known to be haunted*. They were calling out to dead people who never existed there and doing it in an unsafe environment. They did not take the time to study the equipment or stories, research the background of the area or the people who lived there and whose life and death were the basis for their ghostly return. Start with the stories that I have researched or others have delved into and go deeper. You may find some juicy tidbits that help you come into contact with the spirits you seek!

Simple Tools to Seek Out Ghostly Activity

I have listed a few handy and low-cost items if you like to take the stories one step farther and search out the ghosts in this book. Quite honestly, at the very least, a camera and a digital recorder are all you need to explore the haunted side of things. I have seen pretty good ghostly pictures taken with cell phone cameras. When I take photos for my books, I take about a hundred for each place at different angles—not necessarily to catch ghosts, but to get images of the stories' locations so my readers can see where the ghosts haunt. Only every once in a while do I get lucky and find a spirit in one. Most of the time, catching a ghostly image is spontaneous and unexpected. However, I certainly think that if a ghost identifies with you, it is more likely it will notice and hang around you. Regardless, the more images and recordings you take, the more likely you will get a catch a spirit in your camera or a voice in a recorder.

Basic Ghost Tools:

Here you will find the basic ghost searching equipment and a not-so-technical explanation of its use. You can make up an inexpensive kit, if you are on a budget, with an infrared camera and a digital recorder. These are the two simple tools that you can use either night or day or at the spur of the moment.

EMF Detector:

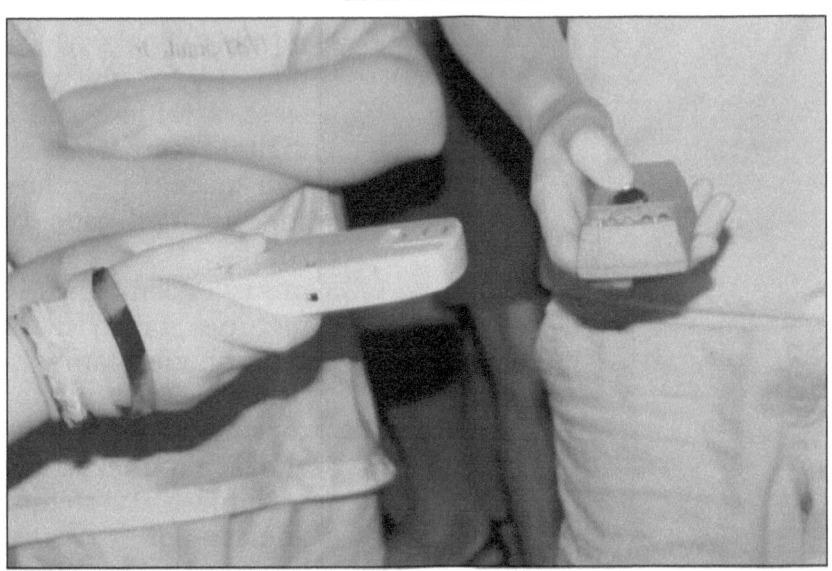

An EMF meter is a scientific instrument measuring fluctuations in electromagnetic fields–invisible lines of force produced by voltage and current. These fields are around us in electronics like computers, lights, televisions, electric cables, and hair dryers. It is a common theory that ghosts contain some electrical residue, or they may be able to disrupt a field of energy. Such, the same kind of spikes that you would get placing an EMF detector near a high electrical outlet could also be used to detect a spirit's presence. EMF detectors, in everyday use, are utilized for tracking and identifying high levels of electronic radiation that could quite possibly be hazardous. If you get a spike on the EMF, it does not necessarily mean there is some ghostly activity. Check for nearby outlets or sources of electricity. Cell phones, wall outlets, and lights can cause a huge spike in the EMF detector.

REM Pod:

Radiating Electro-Magnetic Pod, is a device designed to detect fluctuations in electromagnetic fields. Radiates its own magnetic field. If something gets near it, it makes a loud sound and flashes light.

Digital Recorder:

Digital voice recorders are used to pick up audio not heard with the human ear or to validate audio heard during a session. Be careful in choosing a recorder. Although they are one of the least expensive tools to buy, you want to make sure that it has a way to transfer files from the recorder to a computer for analysis. A recorder with a pop-out USB makes it easy to plug your recorder right into a computer and transfer files for review.

Digital Cameras and Video Recorders:

Digital cameras and video recorders allow the user to see things that are not viewable by the naked eye. Full-spectrum cameras have no filtering, seeing the upper near-ultraviolet, entire-visible spectrum, and near-infrared spectrum. An infrared camera allows users to see into a different light spectrum.

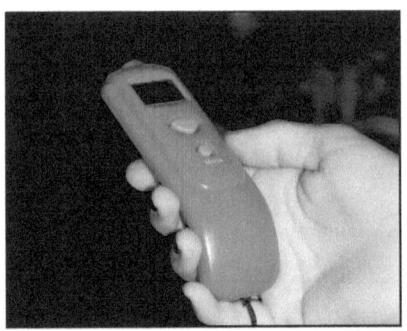

Thermometers:

Digital thermometers allow ghost hunters to see sharp changes in temperatures. These dips and fluctuations could be signs of paranormal activity.

Motion Sensors (infrared or ultrasound):

Motion sensors can detect unusual movement in a region that someone may or may not see with the naked eye.

Spirit Box:

A spirit box is a modified digital radio that sweeps through multiple audio channels, either on AM or FM bands. The user can hear a mix of white noise (static sound) and fragments of chatter like disk jockey voices and music. Many believe spirits can either manipulate words passing through or that the radio waves help the ghost communicate. Listen for clear words and phrases above the jumble of radio sounds.

Thermal Imaging Infrared Camera:

Thermal Imagers work by detecting levels of infrared energy radiating from different objects. They show a map of hot and cool surface temperatures. Different colors are used to distinguish differences in heat signatures in those objects so users can visualize temperature changes in the environment.

Ovilus:

The theory behind the device is that spirits can manipulate the environment so that the ovilus comes up

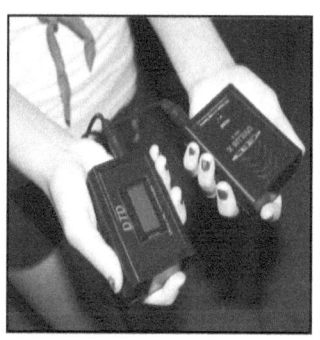

with an appropriate response, converting environmental readings into real words. It has a preset database of words from which to choose. One thing to watch for— many times, the ovilus seems to toss out random words that those listening can manipulate to fit the situation. You have to make sure that you are not just taking the words through the power of suggestion and working a story around your questions.

Trail Camera with Night Vision:

Motion-sensor camera/video camera can be tethered to a tree or set on about any stationary object like a chair. These help cover extended areas during a ghost investigation, cover areas where humans might discourage interaction, or appraise areas before an investigation. The camera is triggered by movement and helps determine if bumping in the attic are flying squirrels banging off the ceiling instead of dead Aunt Ada returning to haunt her next of kin.

A Couple Tools Used Historically

Crystals:

Many tools have been used for centuries to detect fluctuations in the electromagnetic field and can be effective.

Crystals suspended by strings have been utilized since medieval times to find the source of spectral or magical energy. Just as they react to the energy around people, they may also respond to spirit energy.

Dousing or Divining Rods

Dousing or divining rods react to energy. They can be used to find water sources. You can make simple dousing rods out of two metal coat hangers. Gently hold them in your hands, walk across a water source, and watch them move—they are picking up the energy in the water. Then utilize the tool to find spirited energy in an area.

Other Things That Go Bump in the Night

In the outdoors, when the natural and supernatural collide—how do you tell them apart?

Investigating ghosts outside the realms of a closed room can be quite challenging. Outdoors, owls are hooting, coyotes are howling, and bobcats are yowling. If you are near a body of moving water like a stream, they gurgle, rush, and bubble, making humanlike chatter. Dried autumn leaves rustle beneath feet, and tree limbs creak and groan when rubbing together. Ghost hunters in the outdoors must separate natural sources from supernatural ones. And those are just the sounds. Moonshine creeps through leaves and makes strange shadows dancing on the forest floor. If this is not enough to send many ghost-adventurers in the dark of night running for the cover of an old, abandoned house, the very notion that spiders are creeping across the ground, snakes are slithering and ticks are cozying down past your shirt collar just might. It is about researching the wildlife that inhabits the area, knowing the habitat you will be in, and understanding the environment around you that may play tricks on the ears and eyes. When you hear a strange sound, first eliminate any animal it could be—use a recorder to collect the evidence, and then, when analyzing your data, play it back and compare it to wildlife online. If needed, ask a local wildlife authority to identify it. Once you have excluded all natural entities, you may have supernatural evidence!

Common Natural Phenomena to Watch for when Researching Ghosts Outside

Frogs and toads trill and croak, making odd sounds like ghostly children playing.

Ohio has an abundance of animals who venture out of their homes, either night or day. The sounds they make—from calls to footsteps—can deceive those researching ghosts. Here are just a few more common in the region:

Owls: People often misinterpret the hoots, cackles, shrieks, or trilling calls as high-pitched human screams or even ghostly giggles.

Flying Squirrels: They glide from tree to tree chirping and chittering.

Fox and Coyote: Their barks, cackles, and wails are mistaken for demon-like howls.

Deer: Rambling about at night, deer are certainly not known for their ability to see in the darkness and often run into fences and trees, making large crashing sounds. Their footsteps crunch loudly like boots in autumn leaves as loud as human boot steps. They also snort, sneeze, and grunt when surprised.

Insects: Insects tend to buzz by cameras, leaving the same kind of "orbs" in images seen when pictures are taken in Ash Cave and other areas with sand and dirt kicked up by shoes. It is merely a reflection off the insect or, in the caves, sand and dirt.

Bobcat, Skunk, Raccoon, Opossum, and Beaver: These smaller animals are more common in the

Hocking Hills and are inclined to come out at night. They are known to purr, grunt, sniff, and make scratching noises. The crunch of their footsteps in the brush is frequent. Many are not startled so easily, and they will curiously come close to humans.

It is not only animals that catch people off-guard in the out of doors. Plants are known to lead us astray:

Glowing Fungus: A variety of wood-decaying fungus species create bioluminescence (a chemical reaction that makes the plant glow in the dark) called foxfire. It can be seen along trails and especially near old logs. Birds and small mammals may brush against it and glow in the dark!

Creepy Fungus: Dead Man's Fingers, a common fungi, have caught more than a few off-guard! Me, included.

Citations

Athens Insane Asylum
Athens post, December 1, 1978 January 12th
http://www.ohiohistorycentral.org/entry.php?rec=3355
Annual Report of the Secretary of State to the Governor of the
State of Ohio for the year 1886. The Westbote Company, State
Printers 1887
http://www3.interscience.wiley.com/journal/121383843/
abstract—CASE REPORT
Analysis of Suspected Trace Human Remains from an Indoor
Concrete Surface—Carolyn M. Zimmermann, 1 B.S; Ünige A.
Laskay, 1 M.Sc.; and Glen P. Jackson, 1 Ph.D. 1 Center for
Intelligent Chemical Instrumentation, Department of Chemistry
and Biochemistry, Ohio University, Athens, OH 45701-2979.
Image of Dr. Walter Freeman: Courtesy of Lisa Wallerrogers
Fairfield County Hauntings
www.ohioexploration.com/fairfieldcounty.htm ID: 9332160
Level: 1
General Fairfield County and Lancaster City: Moyer, Tad.
True Tales of Fairfield County. Bremen: Bremen Historical
Society, 1987.
Wessa, Pauline. "Library Compiling the Chilling History of
Fairfield Ghosts."
Columbus Citizen-Journal 7 Nov. 1980, pp. 4.
Herbert M. Turner
(2007)
Mary Mulhaney:
The Jackson Standard (Jackson, Ohio) · Thu, Mar 25, 1880
Lyons Falls:
https://www.ohiogenealogyexpress.com/ashland/
ashlandco_hist_1901/ashlandco_hist_1901_pg_009.htm
Haydenville Tunnel
Kings Station—Ghost Town
Frank Mace archives—December 1961
Vinton County Historical Society—Alice's House
Athens Messenger, June 1878
Lake Alma:
History of Lake Alma, Ryan Griffith & Debbie Griffith
Moonville Tunnel:
Frank Mace Archives, 1961
Mike Shea Archives, 1959-1961
Vinton County Historical Society—Alice's House
Athens Messenger, 2/17/1876
Athens Messenger, May 20, 1880
Athens Messenger and Herald, September 1907
McArthur Democrat, March 31, 1859
Athens Messenger, July 17, 1873
Athens Messenger, Thursday November 11, 1880
The Portsmouth Times, December 27, 1938
Athens Messenger, Thursday, October 16,1873
Moonville Tunnel:
—Quackenbush, J. (2017). Moonville. Its Past. Its Ghosts. Its Legends. 21
Crows Dusk to Dawn Publishing
—The Fort Wayne Weekly November 10th 1880
—Athens Messenger, Thursday, Nov 11, 1880
—February 1895 Chillicothe Gazette
White Lady Point

Andrew Henderson, ForgottenOH.com Darby-Lee Cemetery: Ohio Ghost Hunter Guide VIII –Jannette Quackenbush

Elmore Rider:
—The News Messenger Fremont June 11,1927
—Cleveland Plain Dealer November 24, 1922
—The News Messenger Fremont Sep 21, 1942

Louisa Catherine Fox:
—Coshocton Age September 24, 1869 -Almost A Suicide
—The Herald And Torch Light (Hagerstown, Md) February 17, 1869—A Terrible Tragedy in Ohio
—New Philadelphia Ohio Democrat 2/12/1869— Young Girl's Throat Cut By Her Lover—The Murderer Attempts Suicide
—Hagerstown Mail Hagerstown Maryland February 5, 1869
—Greencastle Weekly Indiana Press March 30, 1870—The Scaffold
-- Caldwell, J. A. (1880). History of Belmont and Jefferson counties, Ohio: And incidentally historical collections pertaining to border warfare and the early settlement of the adjacent portion of the Ohio Valley. https://archive.org/details/historyofbelmont00cald/page/n413/mode/2up?q=egypt.
Ohio. State Board of Health. (1900). Third report of an investigation of the rivers of Ohio as sources of public water supplies: 1900.

Old Man's Cave:
—The Hocking Sentinel. June 22, 1905. The Wonderland of Hocking Dead Man's Cave
—Logan Hocking Sentinel July 21, 1853
—The Hocking sentinel., June 22, 1905, Image 4 old man hid money

Mary Stockum:
—Ancestry.com—Stockum
—www.sleepyhollowpumpkins.com/legend_marystockum.htm
—www.graveaddiction.com/stockum.html
—1870 US Census—Linton Twp, Coshocton County
—Profile by Joanna Ross. (1967, Nov 11) Coshocton Tribune
-Map: Linton Township, Bacon P.O., Maysville, Plainfield P.O., Jacobsport Atlas: Coshocton County 1872

Mary Seneff Ghost:
—

Lick Road:
—https://creepycincinnati.com/2019/10/13/lick-road-and-the-legend-of-amy/
—http://www.weirdus.com/states/ohio/road_less_traveled/lick_road/index.php

Cherry Fork Cemetery:
—Cleveland Plain Dealer, Historical Archives August 12, 1896 A Grave Yawns.
—The News-Herald. Hillsboro, Oh. January 18, 1894. Couldn't Get His Breath
—News-Herald. Hillsboro, Oh. Thursday December 27, 1893 Parker Confesses
—The Evening World. New York, NY. January 12, 1894, BROOKLYN LAST EDITION, HANGED BY BEST CITIZENS. Boy Murderer Victim of Mob Law in Ohio
—The News-Herald. Hillsboro, Oh. December 28, 1893, Page 5. An Awful Double Crime
—The Evening Bulletin. Maysville, KY. December 27, 1893.

Bloody Bridge:
—The Bloody Bridge- Old Papers Recall Bloody Tragedy in the Palmy Days of the Canal. May 15th, 1908 Delphos Daily Herald Newspaper

Buckland Lock/Lock 44:
—Akron Daily Democrat. July 21, 1902, Page 5. A Weird Tale of the Canal Locks Near Napoleon

Beaver Creek State Park:

—Ira F. Mansfield; Robin Hood Club. Little Beaver River valleys, Penns— Ohio with illustrated check list of flowers and essays. 1914
—The Legend of Gretchen's Lock. (n.d.). Retrieved from https:// www.carnegie.lib.oh.us/gretchen

Dead Man Hollow:
—Portsmouth Times May 31, 1948 . Grave In the 'Wilds' Of Scioto Co Holds Secret
—Harry Knighton, "Shawnee Forest," undated typescript, Digital History Lab Collection, Clark Memorial Library, Shawnee SU, Portsmouth, Ohio.

Goll Woods:
—genealogy.com/forum/regional/states/topics/oh/fulton/193/

Deep Cut:
—31 Oct 1991, 8 - The Times Recorder Deep Cut Ghost

Hatchet Man:
—September, 1839—Washington Globe Nov. 28, 1840
—Washington Globe April 26, 1843

Red Brick Tavern:
—Red Brick Tavern: files.usgwarchives.net/pa/berks/history/family/ tall0003.txt historicredbricktavern.com/

Witch's Grave:
—(n.d.). The Akron Beacon Journal Akron, Ohio Monday, July 29, 1963 - Page 42. Mike Patton--Portage's Lost Cemetery Surrounded by Mystery.
—Dealing With The Dead: Mortality and Community in Medieval and Early Modern Europe. (2018). Leiden, Netherlands: BRILL.
—Mulford B. Elliott. (n.d.). Retrieved from https://www.findagrave.com/ memorial/35688660/mulford-b_-elliott
—"Remember Me As You Pass By". (n.d.). Retrieved from https:// www.vastpublicindifference.com/2010/02/remember-me-as-you-pass- by.html
—THE INFAMOUS WITCH'S GRAVEYARD. (n.d.). Retrieved from https:// www.flickr.com/photos/129609706@N02/39996617045

Salem Reformed Cemetery:
—Baker, J. (n.d.). Local history: Spooky tales surround the headless angel of Saltillo. Retrieved from timesreporter.com/news/20171030/local- history-spooky-tales-surround-headless-angel-of-saltillo
—Meet the Holmes County ghosts Angel of death at Salem Cemetery, old man who lives in a hotel an. (n.d.). Retrieved from https://www.the-daily -record.com/article/20071028/LIFESTYLE/310289498

Blue Bridge:
—Charles Parker's War of 1812 Blockhouse: The Historical Record and the Terry Speer Collection of Historic Artifacts. (n.d.). Retrieved from https:// www.academia.edu/41001242/ Charles_Parkers_War_of_1812_Blockhouse_The_Historical_Record_and_ the_Terry_Speer_Collection_of_Historic_Artifacts
—The Haunting at Bluebridge - Researching one of the Firelands' Ghosts. (n.d.). Retrieved from https://goth.net/forums/viewtopic.php?t=1666
—History of the Fire lands, comprising Huron and Erie Counties, Ohio, with illustrations and biographical sketches of some of the prominent men and pioneers : Williams, W. W. (William W.) : Free Download, Borrow, and Streaming : Internet Archive Page 254. (n.d.). Retrieved from https://archive.org/details/historyoffirelan00will/page/n323/ mode/2up/search/seymour

Ghostly Hounds:
Cleveland Plain Dealer. (Cleveland, Oh) Historical Archives. February 9, 1895. Followed By Ghostly Hounds

www.ingramcontent.com/pod-product-compliance
Lightning Source LLC
Chambersburg PA
CBHW021014180626
46814CB00003B/1277